"Tell me y...

Jordan's deep velvet voice sent a warm little shiver down her spine. "I'd like you to kiss me," she said. When his gaze dipped to her mouth, her lips parted in invitation. When he hesitated, she leaned out of the tub to grab his tie and pulled him close.

"Now, Jordan."

"It's your fantasy," he whispered, before pressing his lips seductively against hers, his hand dipping beneath the surface of the bathwater to brush against her rib cage. Her head spun, her mind whirled with sensation as he cajoled her tongue to mate with his in a kiss more erotic than anything she'd ever experienced. She moaned when he palmed her breast in the warmth of his large hand. Heat, hot and blazing, built inside her as his thumb lightly teased her nipple into a taut peak.

Suddenly, he stopped. "We can't do this, Cait." He stood and walked over to pick up his jacket, leaving her wanting him, needing him....

"This isn't exactly how I envisioned my fantasy ending," she said, her voice still husky with desire.

"This isn't the end, sweetheart. It's just the beginning." He graced her with a grin guaranteed to speed up her pulse. "By the way, you might want to add a few more bubbles to your bath."

Dear Reader,

Writing can be such a solitary existence and if it wasn't for the support of one of my closest friends, fellow Temptation author, Janelle Denison, Cait and Jordan's romance would never have seen the light of day. The Fantasy for Hire books are a project close to my heart because it finally gave Janelle and I the opportunity to work together. The result of this collaboration—the McBride brothers, two gorgeous, sexy men who've captured our hearts and hopefully, will capture yours as well.

Janelle and I have wanted to team up on a special project for years. Thanks to the encouragement of our editors, Birgit Davis-Todd and Brenda Chin, we were given the opportunity to fulfil a long-awaited fantasy of our own. I hope you enjoy both Temptation #759 *Christmas Fantasy* and Temptation #767 *Valentine Fantasy*.

I'd love to hear from you, so feel free to write to me at P.O. Box 224, Mohall, ND 58761.

Enjoy,

Jamie Denton

VALENTINE FANTASY
Jamie Denton

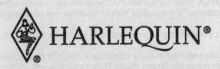

HARLEQUIN®

TORONTO • NEW YORK • LONDON
AMSTERDAM • PARIS • SYDNEY • HAMBURG
STOCKHOLM • ATHENS • TOKYO • MILAN • MADRID
PRAGUE • WARSAW • BUDAPEST • AUCKLAND

Tony,
You're *my* fantasy come true.
Love, Jamie

ISBN 0-373-25867-4

VALENTINE FANTASY

Copyright © 2000 by Jamie Ann Denton.

Visit us at www.romance.net

Printed in U.S.A.

Prologue

"Sex for hire?" Cait Sullivan asked, lowering her voice to a hushed whisper. "Are you serious?"

With the critical eye of a reporter, Cait examined the man across her desk. The expensive suit and Italian loafers were apparel that bespoke money, and not the garb of some crackpot. If she ignored the small bandage across his nose and the fading double shiners that made him resemble a jaundiced racoon, his face didn't look as if it belonged to a crazy, either, but maybe someone who'd had his nose broken.

"I'm perfectly serious, Ms.—" he glanced at her nameplate, then slid his pale blue gaze back to her "—Sullivan. I know for a fact that a representative of Fantasy for Hire was paid to have sex with a client. A very wealthy client."

Cait's instincts kicked into high gear. There was a story here, a good story that wouldn't require her to dress up and play nice with the debutantes of San Francisco—spoiled little girls who made her feel gauche and out of place. It might even keep her away from the boring charity auctions of the rich and infamous, another assignment she found distasteful. This was a *real* story. And if she could pull off the exposé Louden Avery kept hinting at, it might just mean the end of the fluff she'd been writing for the past two years and push her into the type of reporting she craved—hard-hitting news. Investigative reporting. Maybe even move her out of print and into live, on-location shots with one of the networks, or even CNN.

This is Cait Sullivan reporting live...

She tucked the fantasy away and pulled out a yellow pad instead. First things first. "What proof do you have?"

"One of my former employees obtained the—shall we call them *services*," he said, his voice dripping with innuendo, "of Fantasy for Hire. I have no physical proof but I did see a one-thousand-dollar receipt for services rendered. That's a bit steep for a male exotic dancer, wouldn't you agree?"

She'd never personally hired an exotic dancer, but she'd been to a few bachelorette parties and pretty much guessed what these guys did for a living cost nowhere near what he was suggesting.

From what Avery had told her thus far, Fantasy for Hire was a rather small, albeit successful, agency that hired out male strippers for bachelorette parties, birthday parties and the like—something he insisted was merely a front for a more lucrative business.

"I need more than your telling me you saw a receipt, Mr. Avery," she said, making notes on the pad.

"You're a reporter. Isn't it your job to find out the truth behind what I'm telling you?"

"Well, yes, but..."

He stood and looked down his bandaged nose at her. "If you don't want the story, Ms. Sullivan, I'll go to the *Examiner*. I'm sure they'd be interested." He turned to leave.

"Wait!" She stood and circled the desk, unwilling

to let her chance to prove herself as a serious reporter slip away. "Give me a few days to check it out and get back to you. If I think there's a story, we'll talk again."

He smiled, but it was more of a feral grin. "Oh, there's a story, one hell of a story, and I'm giving it to you, Ms. Sullivan."

She didn't want to question why he'd approached her when there were dozens of other reporters on the *Herald* with more experience. Who was she to look a gift horse in the mouth, as her mother would say?

She took the business card he offered and promised to call him in a few days. Propping her backside against the desk, she bit her lip and watched him walk away. Her mind spun with ideas, but nothing concrete took root. She needed something, some glimmer of proof that Avery was telling her the truth, before she spent hours investigating this agency.

With a sigh, she pushed off the desk and returned to her chair to examine her notes. She read through them twice until a slow grin tugged her lips. Drumming her short nails on the desk, her smile turned into a grin and she laughed. She had it! The perfect cover. A foolproof plan. What better way to discover the truth about Fantasy for Hire than to hire the agency herself?

She made a quick call to Ardell's Body Works and begged the receptionist to work her into the schedule. After a few pleas, Hilary relented if Cait promised to be there within the hour. She needed a trim anyway, she thought, but with luck, Pierre could at least tame her hair into a semblance of sophistication and style. Maybe she'd even get her nails done. Rich women got their nails done all the time. She needed to look pampered and bored, and if anyone in the city could achieve that look for her, it'd be the wizards at Ardell's.

Snagging her purse and raincoat, she left the cubicle and hurried across the busy newsroom to the sign-in board. She plucked the red peg from "in" and popped it into the "out" slot under her name, then left the office, ready to set the wheels in motion for her own private fantasy for hire.

1

JORDAN MCBRIDE HAD BEEN sure the impetuousness of youth was far behind him, until he stepped in to handle his younger brother's booming business. Of all the stupid, idiotic things he'd done in his life, agreeing to temporarily run Fantasy for Hire until his brother, Austin, returned from his honeymoon and finalized the sale of the agency topped the list.

With a self-deprecating sigh of disgust, he examined the schedule spread over the scarred mahogany desk. Somehow he'd managed to double-book two of Austin's employees for Valentine's weekend. Although the lovers' holiday was still a week away, his attempt to reschedule had failed. Both customers he'd spoken to had been adamant; if Fantasy for Hire couldn't deliver the appropriate fantasy at the scheduled time, they'd be forced to look elsewhere.

"Great," Jordan muttered before taking a sip from the steaming mug of coffee. He'd been at the helm for less than forty-eight hours and already Austin's customers were threatening to jump ship. If things kept up at this rate, by the time Austin and his bride returned, Fantasy for Hire would be a distant memory.

The phone, which had been ringing nonstop all morning, jangled again. He set his coffee on the blotter, picked up the phone and took an order for a fantasy fireman to perform for the thirtieth birthday of a secretary during office hours. He bet the stuffy partners of the financial-district firm were going to be less than thrilled to have a woman's fantasy come to life in their midst.

The front doorbell rang and he waved the visitor into the house without taking his attention from the order form. At least the financial-district fireman wasn't needed for another three weeks, well after the Valentine's Day rush. He still couldn't believe how many couples married on the holiday for lovers. All fourteen of Austin's employees were booked solid for bachelorette parties, and he still hadn't found a solution to the double booking. One thing he knew for certain, he definitely would not be filling the void. Handling the office portion of his brother's agency was one thing, but playing the role of male exotic dancer was out of the question. A man had to draw the line somewhere, and taking off his clothes for money was a pretty solid line as far as he was concerned.

He finished the call, assured the customer the fantasy fireman would arrive as scheduled, then leaned back in the worn leather chair. He dropped the pen on the desk and turned his attention to the woman who looked nothing like the UPS delivery man he'd expected to find. She stood with her back to him, admiring the Charles Fracé wildlife print he'd given to Austin for Christmas.

He admired *her*.

Legs. Sweet heaven, they were long, not to mention perfectly shaped. The kind of legs that made a man take notice. Black high-heeled pumps and sexy black nylons with seams running up the back didn't hurt either. He followed the line with his eyes until it disappeared beneath the hem of her short black skirt, wondering if lacy elastic tops held them secure, or if she wore one of those sexy little garter belts with satin and bows. Black satin. With little bows the color of ripe, summer strawberries.

He cleared his throat, more to tighten the rein on his runaway imagination than to gain her attention. She turned around anyway, and gave him a smile capable of melting the polar ice caps.

"Hi," she said in a soft, husky voice that set his imagination into overdrive again. Eyes the color of emeralds peered at him from beneath dusky lashes. A halo of russet curls framed a girl-next-door face complete with creamy complexion and a delicate dusting of freckles across the bridge of her nose. She looked the type more comfortable in blue jeans and sneakers ready for a hike over a mountain trail, but he appreciated those sexy, black-seamed nylons just the same.

He stood and circled the desk. "Can I help you?"

Her smile wavered slightly and her gaze darted to the door. She took a deep breath, drawing his attention to the rise and fall of very full breasts beneath a teal silk blouse. "I have a fantasy."

Yeah, so did he!

"Then you've come to the right place," he said, forcing his mind on business instead of black satin and strawberries.

He indicated the metal folding chair, then waited until she was seated before returning to his own behind Austin's old desk. What had once been the family dining room of his youth had been transformed

into a makeshift office that served as the backbone of
Fantasy for Hire, the agency his brother had begun a
few years ago to help pay off school debts. A pair of
old file cabinets that looked as if they'd been pur-
chased at an army-surplus store replaced the antique
china hutch that had belonged to his grandmother
McBride. The oak dining table had been exchanged
for a scarred mahogany desk, and the Tiffany lamp
that had once hung from the ceiling had been replaced by a functional ceiling fan with overhead
lighting. The no-frills office wasn't exactly the type of
place appropriate for receiving visitors or conducting
business in person, but the agency wasn't exactly the
type to invite clientele into its office either.

"Wait a minute. Our address isn't listed in the
phone book. How'd you find us?" Nor was the address listed on the business cards the dancers passed
out at the various parties and functions they attended. Considering the type of entertainment the
agency provided, only their phone number was ad-
vertised in the book.

She offered him a sheepish grin while pushing a
wayward curl behind her ear with a long tapered
nail. "I have a friend with the phone company, and
she checked out your agency for me."

He didn't like the idea that just anyone could ob-
tain the address of an unlisted private residence.
"What specifically can Fantasy for Hire do for you,
Ms...."

"Sullivan. Cait Sullivan," she said in a husky feminine voice that made him think of whispered words
shared between lovers beneath a starry night sky.

He wrote her name on a form, then filled in the

blanks with the Pacific Heights address she provided, along with her phone number. So much for her being the girl next door. Pacific Heights kept the daughters of San Francisco's elite closeted from mingling with the rest of everyday society. Only a pedigree to rival royalty could breach the gated walls. No doubt Ms. Cookies-and-Cream, with her black-seamed stockings, was just bored and looking for a little excitement.

"Our prices are competitive. I don't think you'll find a better bargain in San Francisco to fulfill your needs. Why don't you tell me your fantasy."

She blushed prettily, just a slight coloring that turned her creamy cheeks a soft peach. Lord, she was adorable, and for the flash of an instant, he wished she wasn't a potential client for his brother's business or a part of San Francisco society. But a casual fling held little appeal, and he didn't have the time to pursue his attraction to her in any serious way since he had a career to rebuild.

She set her purse on the floor beside her, then changed her mind and hauled the bag back into her lap. "I need a Valentine for my parents' anniversary party next weekend," she said, twisting the strap around her hand.

Jordan hated to disappoint her, but there was no way he could help her with a Valentine stripper. "This weekend? That's impossible."

"I can afford your—" she cleared her throat "—agency."

"That's not the problem," he said. "I have no one available." He stood, ready to show her to the door, but something in her voice stopped him.

"I really need your help," she said, her eyes matching the plea of her words. "It's my parents' fortieth anniversary and my sisters, older brother and I are having this huge party for them. I *need* a date for the party."

She was mistaken. The agency wasn't an escort service that provided fantasy *dates*. He wasn't suspicious of what she had in mind, but Jordan was well aware that escort services were often a front for prostitution. Austin's motto was fantasy equals seduction of the *mind*. Sure, he provided exotic dancing, but Austin had firm rules—no stripping below the waist and no touching. Most importantly, the guys who worked for his little brother's agency knew their number-one priority was to create a fantasy capable of making a woman catch her breath.

"I wish I could help you, but it's out of the question," he said.

She lowered her gaze, but not before he noted the disappointment in her eyes. Why did he feel as though he'd just kicked a puppy? He didn't even know this woman.

He circled the desk and propped his backside against the edge. Curious, he studied her for a moment. "Why would *you* need a date?" he asked. Better yet, why would someone as adorable as her feel she had to *pay* for one? This was not a woman who should need to pay anyone to take her anywhere. She was stunning. Considering she'd had the ingenuity to track down the agency's address told him she was no wallflower. She was definitely the type to know what she wanted and had the determination and intelligence to accomplish her goals.

She bit her lip and looked up at him. After a moment, a slight grin tugged her lips. "I don't want any entanglements, and my parents would be thrilled if they believed I was dating again, especially since it is Valentine's Day." She looked him up and down. Then she smiled, one of those full, bright smiles she'd flashed him when she first walked into the house. "What about you?"

He frowned. "Me?"

She shrugged. "Sure, why not?"

"I...but we..." don't do dates, he thought. But Austin had. Not only had his brother gone on several dates with Teddy Spencer, he'd fallen head over heels in love with her. Two days ago, they'd eloped.

Maybe Fantasy for Hire did provide the type of service Cait Sullivan wanted and he just wasn't aware of it. He wished he'd paid more attention to his brother's business venture, but he'd been too busy building his own career as an architect to take more than a cursory interest and then issue a string of warnings. He'd always been protective of Austin, and when their parents died unexpectedly when he was eighteen and Austin only sixteen, he'd been left to raise his brother. Though he'd lived in Los Angeles for the past eight years, looking out for Austin was a habit he'd never relinquished, much to his younger brother's irritation.

"Money is no object," she blurted out. To express her point, she fished through her bag and pulled out a small stack of hundred-dollar bills.

He stared at the wad of cash, held securely by her long, red, tapered nails. Austin might be in the process of selling the business, but how could Jordan in good conscience turn down such a hefty commission, even though Cait obviously misunderstood the purpose of the agency? Fantasy for Hire wasn't an escort service, but neither could he walk away from that kind of cash. Money was money and he and Austin had too many lean years behind them for him to ignore what she was practically throwing in his lap.

She wasn't asking him to take off his clothes. He didn't have any plans for next Saturday night anyway, unless it involved an action video and a bowl of popcorn. He'd only been back in San Francisco for a few months and his social calendar was remarkably clear. What harm could there be in standing in as a Valentine for a beautiful woman who piqued his interest?

He sighed. Damn, Austin. His brother was going to get an earful when he returned. "All right," he said, his voice filled with resignation. "You've got yourself a Valentine."

Her smile never wavered, and her eyes brightened considerably as she handed him the cash. "I...uh...I want the full treatment."

He quickly counted the cash, then set the bills on the desk next to the order form. Two thousand dollars! "Full treatment?" he posed tentatively, almost afraid to ask. For two grand, anything was possible.

She stood and slowly moved toward him. "Yes, Mr. Valentine," she said in that husky voice that made him take notice. The tip of her tongue darted out and she moistened her lower lip.

He swallowed. Hard.

"I want the works." She extended her hand toward him. "Do we have a deal?"

He looked at her outstretched hand, and those long, red nails he imagined wrapped around some very interesting places, then over at the cold, hard cash. Regardless of the fact that Austin's wife worked, getting married meant additional financial demands on his brother, and Jordan was certain he'd end up being Uncle Jordan to some adorable kids within a few years. Austin was a family man now. There was no way Jordan could turn down Cait's offer, or ignore the crisp one-hundred dollar bills she'd just handed him.

He took her hand, surprised by the firmness of her grip. "Jordan McBride, valentine for hire at your service. I hope I don't disappoint you."

She pulled her hand from his and gave him a look filled with sexy promise. "I'm sure you won't," she said, hiking his temperature a notch or two.

She left after promising to phone him later in the week with the details for Saturday night.

A valentine!

Why would a woman pay him two grand to be her valentine? And what on earth did she mean by the works? Was she expecting the traditional candy and flowers? Certainly she expected much more, considering the cash she'd paid him.

The phone rang, interrupting his thoughts. He took another order, this time for a fantasy pirate, for the following month. By the time he finished the call, he still hadn't a clue as to what Cait had meant by the works.

Austin's business was fantasies. Women used the services of Fantasy for Hire to fulfill a particular fantasy, whether it was a cowboy, fireman or even an uptight executive type. The business that had been started to help Austin and a few of his buddies pay off their college loans had grown. Its success was due in particular to his brother's vision of a class act, a rule he insisted be followed to the letter.

He went to the kitchen to pour himself another cup of coffee and looked out the bay windows of the breakfast nook to the backyard, still racking his brain about Cait's reference to "the works." When Austin had been hired for Teddy's birthday celebration, he'd given her a Stetson to complete her cowboy fantasy. Maybe that's what Cait wanted. Maybe she was paying him to really *be* her valentine. Maybe she expected candy, flowers and an entire range of small gifts and surprises designed to live up to the agency's motto of the ultimate fantasy, the ultimate mental seduction.

He sipped his coffee, constructing and discarding a variety of ideas worthy of the sum of money he'd been paid. If Cait Sullivan's fantasy was to have herself a valentine, and she was willing to pay for it, then he'd just have do his part in making certain the customer's satisfaction was guaranteed.

"How does anyone do anything with these blasted nails?" Cait muttered as she corrected another typo. She was going to have to do something about them. She could barely function, let alone type.

"Okay, so who is he?"

Cait looked up from her computer to the smiling face peeking over the wall of her cubicle. "What are you talking about?" She frowned at Jennifer Harding, the *Herald's* entertainment reporter and her closest friend.

Jen hurried around the three-quarter wall and dropped into the chair opposite Cait's desk. "The hair, the new makeup, and those god-awful dragon-lady nails. Has to be a *man*."

"It's not a man." Well, maybe it was, but not the way Jen meant. She hit the Save button on the computer and closed the file with her notes on her first meeting with Jordan McBride. She was unsure whether to share with Jen the news about her sideline as an investigative reporter. Not that she questioned Jen's loyalty, but her longtime friend had a tendency toward being overprotective—and extremely nosy.

Jen drummed her nails on the arm of the gray cloth chair. "What's with the getup?"

Cait shrugged. "I wanted a change."

"Ha! The only time a woman wants a change is when she's been dumped or there's a new man in her life. Since you haven't had a steady boyfriend in over a year, that leaves only one other option. Who is he?"

Cait sighed and ignored the gleam in her friend's dark brown eyes. "There's no one. Can we change the subject, please?"

"Okay, so you're not ready to share," Jen teased, adjusting her thick raven hair over her shoulder with a gentle flick of the wrist. "I can respect that."

Cait rolled her eyes, then reached for the folder with her notes on a fund-raiser being held in two weeks. She winced when her clawlike nails caught the end of the plastic in-box. She really had to have these things shaved down to a workable length before she hurt someone. "Did you want something specific, or were you in the mood to harass someone and I'm your unfortunate target?"

"There's a new play in town opening this weekend and I'm reviewing it. Wanna tag along?"

"I can't."

"Ah-ha!" Jen laughed. "I knew it was a man."

Cait set the file on the desk in front of her. Carefully, so she didn't stab herself, she clasped her hands together. "It's my parents' fortieth anniversary this weekend and we're throwing a party for them, or did you forget?"

Jen sighed dramatically. "No. I didn't forget. I'll try to stop by after the play, but I can't promise anything. Do you have a date for the party?"

She thought of Jordan McBride, his rich sable hair and those pale hazel eyes that had swept over her, along with the shiver she'd had a hard time suppressing when he'd looked at her. He could definitely be filed in the drop-dead-gorgeous category with his wide shoulders, lean hips and athletic body. But his eyes drew her attention and held her. Lordy, they were the kind of eyes that could hold a woman spellbound for hours. If Fantasy for Hire really was in the business of seducing wealthy women out of their fortunes as Louden Avery had implied, then Jordan McBride was no doubt a success at his chosen profession. All the man had to do was smile and flash his sexier-than-sin eyes and women would blissfully hand over their wealth.

"As a matter of fact, I do," she admitted.

Jen crossed her arms over her chest and gave her an I-told-you-so look. "I knew it was a man."

"It's not what you think." Cait stood and pulled

her raincoat from the peg behind her desk. "It's strictly business. Let's get some cappuccino. My treat."

"This must be good if you're buying."

Cait glared at her friend. It wasn't that she was cheap, but she'd been taught the value of a dollar by her parents. Spending the money for her new look and the money to hire McBride hadn't been an impulse. She thought of it more as an investment in her future. Her future as a real reporter.

By the time they crossed the street to the Higher Grounds coffee shop, placed their order and found a table in the back, Jen was prodding Cait with more questions. "Tell me about him," she demanded, dipping the edge of her biscotti in her cup of latte.

Cait sipped her cappuccino, then set the cup aside. "I told you. It's business."

"Business? On Valentine's Day?" Jen shook her head with mock dismay. "Honey, we need to have a little talk. You know what they say, all work and no play..."

"Will help me reach my goals sooner?" Cait finished.

Jen set the cookie aside and leaned forward. "Tell me about this business date. Is he gorgeous?"

Cait bit her lip. She knew she could trust Jen, and she was dying to talk to someone about her discovery, even if it meant a well-meaning lecture. Gorgeous didn't begin to explain Jordan McBride. "Gorgeous has nothing to do with this. He's a story."

"Borrrrrringgg. More tales of the rich and famous."

Cait shook her head. "Not this time." This time, she had a lead on a real story, a story that would have her editor, Edmund Davidson, : nd up and take notice. She was convinced if she broke the story on Jordan McBride, Edmund would seriously consider moving her into investigative reporting. He continually told her she was too young, she needed more life experiences. How on earth did he expect her to gain experience if he kept sending her to debutante balls and fund-raisers? Last week she'd been assigned the opening of another art gallery funded by a bored housewife of some Montgomery Street financial wizard. Not exactly hard-hitting news as far as she was concerned.

"Oh?" Interested, Jen propped her chin in the palm of her hand. "Tell me more."

Cait looked around the coffeehouse, making sure they wouldn't be overheard, then very quickly explained her meeting with Louden Avery the previous afternoon and his claims against Fantasy for Hire.

"So, I hired myself a date for my parents' party," she finished, raising her cappuccino in mock salute. "I need the inside scoop and what better way to accomplish that than hiring my own fantasy?"

Jen sipped her latte then set the cup back on the Formica table. "How much did this fantasy date cost the paper?"

"Nothing. I took the money out of my savings account. If the story pans out like I think it's going to, I'll put it on my expense account."

"How much?" Jen asked again, frowning.

Cait knew her friend had only been half teasing about her springing for coffee. They'd been roommates in college and Cait was used to Jen's lighthearted badgering about her ability to squeeze a dollar.

"Jen, it's really not important. What's important is—"

"Cait, how much?"

Cait sighed. She adored Jen, but sometimes her friend was just a little too pushy. She thought about evading the question, but the other woman wasn't a reporter for nothing. "Two thousand dollars," Cait admitted quietly.

"Two thousand! Are you crazy? Cait, what if the story doesn't fly? Then you're out that money."

"Shh, lower your voice." She looked around and was relieved to find no one paying them any attention. "It's okay. I'll get it back."

"Look, kiddo, I know where you work, okay? We're not at the *Herald* because the pay is stellar. The *Chronicle* or *Examiner* we're not."

"Stop worrying, okay? I'm house-sitting for my brother for another few months, so I don't have to worry about rent or utilities. I don't have a car payment. Even if the story doesn't work out and I don't get reimbursed, I'll have the money back in my savings by the time Brian returns from Europe. I'll be fine."

"What are you hoping to gain by this?"

"You know what I want, Jen," Cait said, her voice filled with steely determination. "This story is going to prove to Edmund that I can write real news. If I have to attend one more charity function, I'll scream."

"I just think there's a way for you to do this that doesn't include cleaning out your savings account.

When do you plan on telling Edmund what you're up to?"

"I'm not."

"I wouldn't do that if I were you."

Cait knew her friend was merely concerned for her welfare, but she had to go through with this, on her terms. She couldn't lose this story. "If I tell Edmund, he's either going to take the story away from me and give it to one of the 'boys' or shelve the idea. I can do this, Jen. I can expose Fantasy for Hire. When I handed McBride that money, he jumped on it, so I know there's a story there. By the time I'm finished, this is going to be the biggest scandal to hit the Bay in months."

"I just don't think you've thought this out completely. What makes you think McBride is going to attempt to seduce you out of the fortune you don't have?"

Cait grinned, her enthusiasm mounting. "I have it all worked out. I'm living in Brian's house in Pacific Heights. The party is at the Palace Hotel. He's going to think I've got money."

"There's still a problem. You said that this Avery character claims that this agency was paid for sex. How exactly do you plan on proving *that?*"

"Easy," Cait said, tapping her lengthy acrylic nail on the rim of her cup. "I'm going to seduce Jordan McBride."

2

JORDAN CHECKED his watch, then set aside the designs he'd been studying for most of the afternoon before rubbing at the tension building in his neck. Going into business for himself hadn't turned into the profitable venture he'd imagined, but he had a decent beginning, and that was just fine with him. The desire to work for no one other than himself had been too strong to ignore, and he couldn't complain about the progress he'd made since returning to San Francisco, even if he wasn't yet blazing any trails. He'd done the architectural-firm route in Los Angeles and had been burned, which convinced him he was ready to fly solo. If he'd learned anything during his eight years with Lawrence and Brooks, it was that he wanted his successes, or his failures, to be his own in the future.

Lifting the drawing toward the light, he carefully compared the sketches to the preliminary model for the chain of strip malls planned along the central and northern coast. His presentation for the developer wasn't for a couple of days. He needed to wrap this up as soon as possible so he could start on the actual plans for the Wyndhaven Town House restoration project he'd just been awarded. He'd be buried in meetings with the developer and contractor in another couple of weeks, and he still wanted to bid on a new high-rise complex for downtown. He had some ideas he felt fairly confident about, and the added commissions would give him the capital he needed to hire an assistant and locate reasonably priced office space.

Office space wasn't his only real-estate concern. He and Austin owned the house, but with Austin married, the last thing the newlyweds needed was him around cramping their style. Selling the prime real estate was out of the question. The house had been in the family for three generations, and neither he nor Austin were willing to sell. They could have done so years ago when things had been tough, but they'd made a pact never to jeopardize the house. There'd been times they'd had to survive on canned soup and peanut butter and jelly for weeks, but in the end, the sacrifices more than made up for the cash the house could have brought them. Moving out of the Victorian for Austin and his new bride was Jordan's only logical choice. What he needed to do was find his own place, but he was going to be around until the escrow on his Santa Monica condo closed in a couple of weeks, unless he wanted to throw money away on a rental.

The thought of money brought him back to what he'd been trying to avoid thinking about all afternoon.

Cait Sullivan.

He had a few ideas on how to fulfill her Valentine fantasy, but he still couldn't understand why a woman as attractive as Cait felt she had to pay for the services of a total stranger. She'd mentioned not wanting any entanglements, so perhaps she was recovering from a bad relationship. Anything was possible, he decided, adding another Canary Island pine to the model.

His mind refused to remain focused on his work. Cait and her black-seamed stockings continued to intrude. With a disgusted sigh, he tossed the small pine tree back onto the table. He'd never get any work done at this rate.

He flipped off the light over his desk, and left the upstairs room he'd commandeered as his temporary office space. His real-estate concerns would have to wait until at least next week. His calendar had been filled by a sexy redhead with a fantasy. And for the price he'd been paid, he'd better deliver.

CAIT SNEEZED, dropped the fingernail file, then sneezed again from the dust cloud caused by her vicious filing. She nearly had the length of her new nails down to something she could live with, but her arm ached from the constant, repetitive motion.

Time for a break, she decided, tossing the nail file on the glass end table. She reached for the cardboard container of shrimp fried rice from Mr. Wong's she'd picked up on her way home from the paper. The shrimp was cold, and she blamed it on her nails. They were a serious impediment to her life-style. Not only did she have trouble typing, which was a problem since she wanted to add a few more notes to her story, but attempting to fasten the button fly on her favorite pair of faded Levi's had been impossible. After a ten-minute struggle, she'd given up and slipped into a pair of sweats instead, deciding that if she was going to function and perform the everyday tasks necessary to basic survival, she'd better shave a few millimeters from her fingers first.

She bit into another cold piece of shrimp and thought about the story she was convinced would change the course of her career onto the path she'd craved since she was a little girl. When she'd told Jen her plan, her friend had called her a certifiable idiot, then continued with a list of reasons why she might fail, not to mention a lecture on the danger she was placing herself in by attempting to seduce a total stranger. At the time, she'd waved Jen's concerns aside, but as she dug through the container in search of more shrimp, she couldn't help wondering if perhaps she was letting her ambitions cloud her judgment.

Her plan wasn't exactly foolproof, and she knew it. Like, how did she get around actually having sex with her fantasy date? She'd worry about that later. A good investigative reporter took risks. Woodward and Bernstein had taken a monumental risk in exposing the Watergate scandal, and for a time, their lives had been in danger. Would the savings-and-loan scandal have been exposed if a reporter hadn't ignored the risks involved? Or what about the reporters who put their lives on the line every day to bring news from Kosovo or other war-torn areas? Did those reporters worry about the risks?

No. The story came first. The story *always* came first, and her philosophy was no different from the greats' before her. She knew she'd have to be alone with Jordan, especially since she planned to make it perfectly clear to him that she was on the prowl for seduction. She couldn't very well convince the man that she was ripe for the picking in a roomful of people, especially with her family hovering around her. She'd have to find a way to be alone with him, and although she'd need to brush up on her seductress skills to pull this off, she knew she could do it. In the name of investigative journalism, in honor of the great reporters of years past, she could and would expose Fantasy for Hire.

Setting her shrimp fried rice aside, she picked up the industrial-strength emery board and continued to work on shortening her nails while listening to the evening newscast. More rain was predicted for the Bay area later that week, but the meteorologist promised clear skies by the weekend for Valentine's Day in the most romantic city in North America. She smiled. Not even Mother Nature would dare spoil her parents' anniversary party.

After finishing her nails and waiting for the coat of clear polish to dry, she snapped off the television and flipped on Brian's elaborate stereo system. She found a rock station she liked, then sat down at her laptop computer and popped in the disk containing her notes on Fantasy for Hire.

She carefully read what she'd written during her meeting with Louden Avery. So far, he appeared to be correct in his allegations. The fact that Jordan McBride had taken the huge sum of money she'd offered him led her to believe there was some truth to the claim of money in exchange for sex. Of course, it was up to her to *prove* the claim, but she wasn't too worried about that, even though she had no experience with seducing a man. Flirting, yes. She could handle flirting, but actual seduction? Maybe she'd

better rent a few videos on the art of seduction. Like
The Graduate, she thought with a grimace.

She clicked the icon for a blank page and centered
Jordan McBride's name at the top, then started typing
what she knew about him, which wasn't much. Other
than the fact that he was gorgeous and more than
willing to be her Valentine for a fee, she knew nothing about the man. She didn't know if he owned the
agency, or if someone else pulled the strings behind
the scenes. All she had was Louden's claim that an
employee of Fantasy for Hire took money in
exchange for sex. It was up to her to prove this was a
common practice for the agency.

She pulled up another blank page and made a list
of things she needed to learn about the agency. She
needed to find out who owned the agency, but a huge
help would be a list of previous clients. If she could
find one more person to verify the claim made by
Louden. That, coupled with whatever her own experience with Jordan might produce, would add up to
the necessary verification. Obtaining a client list
would be impossible, unless she crossed the legal line
and resorted to breaking and entering.

She underlined the entry to think about later.

An hour later, she took a short break and headed
for the kitchen for a cup of tea. She was pleased with
her progress. The beginning was already shaping up,
and she had a solid line on which direction she
planned to take the article. As her investigation deepened, so would the depth of her story.

She set the teakettle on the stove, then pulled a mug
from the cabinet as the chimes for the front door rang.
She wasn't expecting anyone, but that never stopped

her nosy sisters from dropping by unannounced. Sometimes having four older siblings could be a royal pain, but she loved them anyway, even if they did think her business was their business.

She strolled to the front door and peered out the side panel to find a Toyota four-wheel drive she didn't recognize parked in the driveway.

"Who is it?" she called.

"It's your valentine," a deep, velvety voice answered from the other side of the door.

Her heart stopped, then resumed at a maddening pace.

Her valentine?

She wasn't supposed to see him until Saturday night. What was he doing here? Unless, she thought, narrowing her eyes, he'd decided she required further investigation as a potential target. She'd struggled hard not to flinch when she'd handed over most of the contents of her savings account. Obviously her plan had worked, and that pleased her. She'd hate to think she'd spent the money for nothing.

"Just a minute," she called, then frantically swiped at the fingernail dust still clinging to her navy sweatshirt. She stifled a sneeze, ran her fingers through her hair in hopes of restoring a sense of order and pinched her cheeks for color. A quick glance down at her clothes caused a groan to escape her lips. What on earth would he think seeing her dressed in baggy sweats, her hair a mess and not an ounce of makeup on her face? So much for playing the socialite. She looked more like the hired help.

Pasting a welcoming smile on her face, she straightened her shoulders and opened the door. Her stomach flipped at the sight of him. Lordy, he was even more drop-dead gorgeous than she remembered. He wore the same navy polo shirt and tan trousers he'd had on earlier, but the worn, leather bomber jacket that matched the color of his wind-tossed, sable hair gave him a slightly dangerous appeal that put her feminine senses on alert.

"Hi," he said, that rumbling voice jarring her back into reality—the reality that Jordan was really standing on her porch.

"I wasn't expecting anyone," she said, taking another swipe at the dust on her shirt. She wanted him to think of her as someone who was polished and sophisticated, not as someone who lounged around the house in dust-covered sweats.

"I hope I'm not interrupting anything important." He looked at her closely, his gaze sliding along her body as if searching for the curves beneath her baggy clothes.

Her temperature shouldn't have heightened just because he looked at her, but it did. Good grief, how did she expect to seduce him when he had her heating up like a furnace with one simple sweep of his gaze?

"Were you sanding something?" he asked, looking closer.

She gave him a quick grin. "Sort of," she muttered, and took a step back. *Just taking precautions so I don't poke your eye out when I get to run my hands through that thick hair of yours.*

"Would you like to come in?" she asked, opening the door wider. If he was here to do a little investigating of his own, she'd be more than happy to oblige.

Besides, maybe she could find an opportunity to learn more about him and the agency.

"I just dropped by to give you this," he said and held out a red velvet, heart-shaped box of chocolates. "From your valentine."

Stunned, she stared at the box, then up at him. She detected a hint of shyness that threw her off-kilter. When she'd first met him, she'd had the impression that Jordan McBride was the type of man who knew exactly what he wanted, and sought it with single-minded determination. She easily imagined him as the high-powered executive type. A take-no-prisoners kind of guy. Of course, she suspected the impression he gave was misleading. Take-the-money-and-run was a more appropriate description.

"Oh." She reached for the beautifully wrapped box. "Oh," she added with a little more emphasis when realization dawned. This had to be part of his plan to seduce her out of her supposed fortune. She recognized the shyness now for what it was—a ploy, a part of the game of seduction. Well, two could play this game.

She graced him with her best sultry smile. "Thank you, Jordan. That's very sweet of you."

A high-pitched wail sounded from the kitchen. "I was making tea," she said, leading him into the house. "Would you like a cup? Or perhaps something a little stronger?"

He hesitated for a moment, then stepped into the foyer. "Tea's fine."

"I heard we're due for more rain," she said. With the box of chocolates still clutched in her hand, she led the way through the house to the kitchen, wishing she could think of something witty or charming to say. She'd attended enough society events, sat through numerous charity functions and listened to endless useless and boring conversations. Couldn't she come up with anything to talk about besides the weather?

"Typical for this time of year," he commented. He sidled up to the breakfast bar and watched as she retrieved another mug from the cabinet. "Nice place. You live here alone?"

Cait blinked. "Uh..." What did she say? She didn't feel comfortable telling a total stranger she lived alone. To do so would violate every rule she'd ever been taught, but this was a business arrangement. She couldn't very well conduct an investigation if she wasn't willing to take risks.

Anything for the story.

"Yes, I do live alone," she said, casting a surreptitious glance in his direction to gauge his reaction.

He nodded, then looked around the enormous, sterile kitchen. White ceramic tiles and white cabinets graced most of the room, the only break in color offered by way of aluminum-topped appliances and a few green plants scattered about. The plants were her touch, not that her brother was ever home long enough to see to their care. Brian had his own computer company and was often away on business.

Cait let out a slow breath, grateful he didn't question her further on her living arrangements. Lying didn't come easily, and she wondered briefly if that character trait would prevent her from becoming an investigative reporter.

No, she decided. She just needed more practice.

She finished preparing the tea, and led him onto the glass-enclosed patio overlooking Brian's extensive ornamental garden. A flick of the switch bathed the sitting area in soft, romantic light, but the highlight was the illumination of the gardens with its variety of flower beds, plants and shrubs, complete with cobblestone bridge and waterfall. Whenever she saw the garden at night, she thought of intimacy and romance. Hopefully, Jordan would, too.

"Very nice," he commented, taking the mug of tea she offered.

"My brother likes gardens," she said, then briefly closed her eyes at her blunder. "So I had one designed for him that looks a lot like this one," she added hastily, with a casual wave of her hand. She'd have to be more careful in the future. "Uh, would you like to see the rest of the house?"

Jordan turned to look out over the garden. "No, this is fine." He hadn't been sure what he'd expected to find by dropping by Cait's tonight with the first of the valentine surprises he'd had planned for the week, but he couldn't help being pleasantly surprised by the girl next door who'd greeted him. He still liked those black-seamed stockings, but she looked adorable right now—like the kind of woman who didn't need the trappings of the social set to be happy, the kind of woman a man could have meaningful and intellectual conversations with, the kind a man looked forward to coming home to after a day at the office.

Bothered by the direction of his thoughts, he turned to find her watching him, her eyes filled with curiosity. She sat on the edge of a white wrought-iron chair, the box of chocolates resting in her lap. She lifted the mug to her lips and looked at him over the rim. "Thank you for the chocolates."

"You're welcome."

She set her mug on the matching table, then untied the satin bow on the heart-shaped box. Carefully, she lifted the lid and placed it on the table next to the mug of tea. She stood, moving slowly toward him, the open box clutched in her hands. "I love chocolates. Don't you?" she asked, her voice low and sultry. He dropped his gaze to her mouth and caught the barest hint of a grin.

"Yeah, chocolate's nice," he said, but he was more interested in the slight curving of her lips and the sweet womanly scent that wrapped around him when she stopped in front of him.

Her tongue darted out and wet her bottom lip. "Would you like a...taste?"

"Taste?" All he could think of tasting was her lips.

She plucked a piece of candy from the box and slowly brought it to her mouth, her eyes never leaving his. Like a sorcerer's spell, her gaze held him, then she bit into the chocolate. She closed her eyes briefly and moaned, a delicate little sound that heated his blood and had his imagination whirring like an overworked power drill.

Jordan could only watch her; he didn't think he could speak if his life depended on it. Sweet heaven, what was she doing to him?

She plucked another chocolate from the box and held it to his lips. He bit into the confection, and her fingers lingered for the briefest instant, lightly brushing his bottom lip. A surge of heat sped through his body at her feathery touch. Oh man, was he ever in trouble.

She held the remainder of the candy in front of him, just out of reach. "So, how long have you been running Fantasy for Hire?"

If she wanted to play siren, he'd gladly cooperate, and enjoy every enticing second. Leaning forward, he took the chocolate in his mouth, then used his tongue to lightly trace the tip of her finger. The green of her eyes darkened and a wave of male satisfaction reared inside him. "Just a couple of days, actually," he said around the candy.

"Really?" She plucked another chocolate from the box. "It's a new business?"

She appeared casual, as if his answer lacked importance, but her eyes told a different story. Mingled amid the heated darkness swirling in the depth of her gaze, he detected a note of curiosity. He didn't know quite what to make of her interest in his brother's agency. Was it simply because she'd hired them to perform an unusual request and she was cautious? Or was there some other ulterior motive to her questioning?

Curiosity, he told himself firmly. Yet, he couldn't help the distrust lurking beneath the surface of his thoughts. After what he'd been through with Lawrence and Brooks, he was bound to be a little cynical. Not everyone had an ulterior motive, and Cait didn't look like the dishonest type. In fact, she looked fresh, sweet and sexy, even if her legs were hidden beneath baggy fleece.

He set his mug on the low table behind him, took the box of candy from her and set it beside the mug.

"It's been around awhile. I'm just handling things while my brother's out of town."

With the caramel-covered chocolate still between her fingers, she moved closer. "Oh. Has your brother been in business long?"

"A few years."

"Fantasy for Hire must be successful."

He lifted her hand with the candy and brought it to her lips. "Take a bite."

Her eyes widened in a startled reaction to his turning the tables on her, but after a brief hesitation she slowly sank her teeth into the caramel. She offered him the remainder, and he took the chocolate into his mouth, circling her finger with his tongue again. She trembled, and his mouth tipped into a smile. Something was happening between them, something that went beyond her hiring him to be her valentine, and he had the distinct impression that whatever it was would have a huge impact on both of them. He hardly knew her, but what little he did know intrigued the hell out of him.

"It pays the bills," he said, resisting the urge to pull her into his arms and taste her sweet mouth. Instead, he took a step back. "I should be leaving."

She drew in a deep breath, looking wary and slightly shaken by their seductive play. He hadn't meant for things to go so far. His intent had been to play a little, turn the tables on her and give her a taste of what she'd been so willing to dish out, but he couldn't help his feeling of satisfaction at the thought of her being affected by him. If the next few days were anything like the last few moments, it was going to be one exciting week.

She turned away, but not before he caught the delicate blush staining her cheeks. He grinned at the switch from seductress to shy girl next door.

She led the way back through the enormous house to the front door. "I'll see you tomorrow," he said, opening the door.

She looked up at him and frowned. "Tomorrow?"

He leaned toward her, his mouth hovering just above hers. The urge to kiss her was strong, and he nearly gave in to the impulse. "Tonight, candy," he whispered. "Tomorrow, the stars."

Instead of her lips, he brushed his mouth across her cheek, then stepped into the night air, hoping the breeze blowing in from the Pacific was cool enough to lower his overheated temperature a degree or two.

"HERE." Cait dropped a small plastic bag filled with chocolates in front of Jen. "Have yourself a party."

She sat in the chair beside Jen's desk, leaned back and closed her eyes. The day had only begun, and already she was exhausted. What sleep she managed to get the night before had been restless at best. She blamed Jordan. Jordan and his blatant, audacious promise of the stars.

"What's wrong with you?" Jen asked over the steady tap of the keyboard.

Cait opened her eyes and looked at her friend. "Chocolate is what's wrong."

Jen laughed and turned to face her. "You have an overdose or something?"

Oh, she'd had an overdose all right, an overdose of sexual attraction that had taken her completely by surprise. "You could say that," she murmured, recalling the heat that had ignited her body and the flash of hunger that had leaped through her like a flame.

She might only be twenty-six years old, but she'd experienced sexual attraction a time or two in her life. There might not be a little black book with evidence of her experience lurking in her past, but she was a far cry from the blushing virgin. Never had anyone made her insides feel so tight and jittery the way Jordan had with one heated look, a whispered word filled with sensual promise, or the chaste brush of his lips against her cheek. She was definitely playing with fire.

"So what's with the chocolate?" Jen asked, bringing her back to the present.

"It was a gift." At her friend's raised eyebrow, she added, "From my valentine."

"Ooh." Jen pushed aside the papers cluttering her desk and braced her elbows on it. Leaning forward, her eyes bright with curiosity, she asked, "The fantasy guy?"

Cait propped her elbow on the desk and rested her temple against her fisted hand. "You won't believe what I did last night," she said, unable to keep the smile from her lips. As she described it, *she* could hardly believe what she'd done to him last night. She explained how her valentine had taken control of the situation, the seduc*ee* becoming the seduc*er*. It stung to admit she'd been brilliantly trapped by her own brazen plan. Her intent had been to garner information, which she'd managed to obtain, and at least she'd learned the identity of the agency's owner. Her investigating had stalled at the point that Jordan had managed to completely enrapture her with his special brand of sensuality.

"I told you this was dangerous," Jen said in her best I-told-you-so voice. "You have to put a stop to this. Demand a refund or something."

Cait sat up straight and looked at her friend. "I can't." And she wouldn't. The story was there, she was sure of it. She wasn't about to stop now, not when she'd had a taste of real investigative journalism. And it had absolutely nothing to do with Jordan's velvet-soft voice and his galactic promise.

The phone on Jen's desk rang, but she ignored it. "Sure you can," she said. "Just tell him something came up, an old friend or a relative from out of town. Something. Tell him you're going to your parents' party with the make-believe relative and forget about this insanity."

Cait shook her head. "No way. I found out last night that the agency's been in business for a while. I need to find out how many other women they've seduced out of their money in exchange for sex."

Jen leaned back in her chair and crossed her arms over her chest. The look she gave Cait was filled with skepticism. "And just how do you plan on doing this?"

Cait pushed out of the chair and stood. She had an appointment in two hours with a representative from the new animal shelter being funded and operated by the elite San Francisco Kennel Club and she still needed to prepare her questions and talk to the photographer scheduled to accompany her. "The wheels are already in motion. I'm just going along for the ride."

Jen frowned, but the concern in her eyes warmed Cait's heart. It was just like Jen to worry.

"You be careful, kiddo."

Cait slung her bag over her arm. "I will. I promise."

She turned to leave but Jen stopped her. "What do you plan on doing next?"

Cait let out a long sigh. "Well, he promised me the stars tonight. I guess I'd better pick up my space suit from the cleaners."

3

HER SPACE SUIT consisted of an electric-blue silk dress more reminiscent of a chemise than outerwear, matching three-inch heels, a delicate gold ankle bracelet and a few strategically placed dabs of her most expensive perfume, a gift from her brother for her last birthday. If Jordan planned to take her to the stars, then Cait had every intention of letting him know she was ready for takeoff.

She applied a light dusting of blush to her cheeks, then finished by thickening her lashes. She blew her hair dry to soften the curls into the more stylish cut fashioned by the wizards at Ardell's, a far cry from her usual easy-maintenance, wash-and-wear style. She completed her ready-for-sin ensemble by adding thin gold hoops to her lobes.

Examining her appearance critically, she smiled at her reflection, confident her valentine would take one look at her and forget about the dust-covered sweats she'd worn the night before. She looked seductive and sexy, and if Jordan McBride couldn't read the signs that said, "I'm ready for a night of passion," then the man was either blind or stupid.

The chimes at the front door signaled his arrival. With one last look, she fluffed her bangs and hurried down the stairs. She smoothed her dress, and tossed her head and shoulders back in an effort to convey a confidence she wasn't quite feeling. Truth be told, her insides were quaking like the California coastline.

She took a deep breath, then slowly opened the door. Resting her hand on the doorjamb above her head, she struck what she hoped was a seductive pose.

"Good evening," she practically purred, waiting for him to turn around to face her. When he did, she smiled, slowly running her gaze up and down his body, praying she gave the impression she was undressing him with her eyes.

Her confidence wavered. For a night of passion, the man had certainly dressed casually. Crisp jeans clung to his lean hips and muscular thighs, while a basic black polo shirt heightened the swirling colors in his pale hazel eyes. The leather jacket she'd admired the previous evening completed his appearance of heading out for a 49ers game.

He raked a shock of sable hair out of his eyes, eyes that held more than an appreciative glint. "You look fabulous," he said in that deep voice that sent a shiver of delight up her spine.

"You look...comfortable." She pushed the door open wide. "Come in."

He grinned, just a slight curving of the lips, but as his eyes swept over her again, her confidence grew at the pleasure in his gaze.

"I thought you might like to go for a walk."

She frowned. "A walk?" She was prepared for him to think she was ready for a night of heavy breathing, and the man wanted to take a walk? In these heels?

Was he nuts? She'd have a blister before they reached the end of the sloped driveway.

He nodded, his grin never faltering. In fact, she thought he looked rather...amused. Not exactly the reaction she'd hoped for. She wanted him thinking of increased heart rates due to deep kisses and tangled limbs, not due to an aerobic workout.

He stepped into the foyer. "Along the wharf," he added, closing the door.

She dropped her hands to her sides. "The wharf? You said something about the stars."

His grin widened, but at least he didn't laugh at her. "I meant a moonlit stroll. What'd you think I meant?"

Oh yeah. That was definitely amusement in his gaze. Her body heated from an embarrassment that had nothing to do with him devouring her with his eyes, but from making a fool of herself. He literally meant the stars, as in astronomy, the galaxy, or the Milky Way, not the culmination of an incredible orgasm.

She blew out a breath harsh enough to ruffle her bangs. "Never mind," she muttered as she headed up the stairs to change into something more appropriate for gazing at stars rather than into each other's eyes.

TWO HOURS LATER, Jordan was in no hurry to bring their evening to an end, so he suggested they grab a bite to eat at one of the more casual seafood restaurants along Fisherman's Wharf. The hostess led them to a table overlooking the ocean, rambled off the dinner specials, then left them to study the menus.

He scanned the list of items, but his mind continued to drift to the first woman in a very long time who'd managed to intrigue him to the point of distraction. He was by no means a monk, but right now, he had difficulty recalling his last serious relationship with a woman. He knew he'd become a workaholic the past few years, and because of his professional ambitions, he'd never taken the time necessary to cultivate a lasting relationship. Most of his contact with the opposite sex had stemmed from one of a multitude of professional acquaintances, but none of the women he'd dated were "the one."

Cait was different. She intrigued him, and he wanted to learn more about her. He found no other plausible explanation for his wanting to extend their evening together.

He glanced in her direction and watched as she surveyed the menu. She nibbled on her bottom lip as she attempted to decide on her meal. Looking up at him, she smiled, then returned her attention to the menu. A slight blush covered her cheeks. She was a contradiction in a variety of ways. Shy, yet temptingly seductive. He didn't think he'd ever know her completely, but he decided that he'd sure like to try once he completed his contractual obligation for Fantasy for Hire.

Tonight he'd seen nary a glimpse of a bored socialite, and he found himself enjoying the company of a fun, carefree woman who grasped life with both hands and enjoyed every moment to the fullest. She'd laughed at the antics of a street mime who'd chosen her as a target for his comedy routine, tossed raw fish off the wharf to the baby sea lions playing on the rocks below, and told him that although she'd lived in San Francisco her entire life, she'd never visited Alcatraz because she couldn't bear the thought of anyone being stripped of their freedom. When they strolled past a New Age shop, she'd explained the various crystals and the power she believed they held, then balked at the overpriced gifts in the window display of a collectibles shop. She was intelligent and witty, but it was not the biting sarcastic wit of someone raised among the privileged, with no conscience about the feelings of others.

Cait cared, a quality he found endearing.

She made him laugh. Something not many were able to achieve.

She was sinfully sexy.

And he wanted her.

"Ready to order?" he asked, closing his menu.

She peeked at him over the top of the menu. "I can't decide between the seafood salad or the giant mushrooms stuffed with shrimp and lobster."

"Order the salad and I'll share my mushrooms with you."

"Deal," she said, then snapped the menu closed. Her smile filled with mischief. "But don't expect me to part with my salad."

He chuckled and signaled for the waiter. "You're a selfish woman, Cait."

She reached for her water glass and took a sip. "You've discovered my weakness."

"Selfishness or seafood?"

She set the glass down, then trailed a short, tapered fingernail along the rim of the crystal goblet. He followed the movement with his eyes and imagined her fingers trailing a path over his chest. He reached for his own water and took a deep drink.

"I'd go to the ends of the earth for seafood," she admitted.

He set his glass aside, braced his arms on the table and leaned toward her. "Is that your only weakness?"

A teasing smile canted her lips and filled her eyes with laughter. "Chocolate," she whispered, lowering her gaze as if embarrassed by the reminder of last night's sensual game.

His blood heated at the memory, and at her display of shyness. He was beginning to think her role of seductress was merely an act, but she'd been just as affected last night as he'd been—another aspect of her personality he found fascinating.

The waiter arrived, and Jordan placed their order, adding a bottle of private-label Chardonnay.

"Make it the house brand," Cait told the waiter, then grinned sheepishly at Jordan. "I'm sorry, I don't like to waste money on an expensive bottle that we won't even finish."

At the waiter's pointed look, Jordan gave a slight nod of agreement. He watched her as she looked out at the ocean lost in thought, more than a little surprised by her frugality, but he figured this was just one of those odd little eccentricities that made up her intriguing personality.

By the time the waiter returned with their wine and poured them each a glass, Jordan surprised himself with the realization he could easily sit and watch the moonlight streaming through the window with her for hours. Only the fact that he wanted to get to know her better prompted him into conversation. "So what do you do for a living, Cait?"

Cait turned to look at him, the truth almost escaping from her lips. "People with trust funds don't work," she managed with a laugh, but the sound held more of a nervous edge than the dismissive tone she'd attempted to achieve. "What about you? Does Fantasy for Hire keep you very busy?"

"I'm an architect."

"An architect?" She might have pictured him as a high-powered executive, but she was still unprepared for his answer. He was part of an agency that allegedly swindled money out of rich women in exchange for sex. He wasn't supposed to be a respectable professional.

"You sound surprised. Don't I look like an architect?" he asked in a low voice that rumbled along her nerve endings.

"It's not that. It's just that...I thought you worked exclusively for your brother."

He laughed. "Fantasy for Hire is Austin's brainchild. I'm merely the reluctant hired help for about a week."

Reluctant because he didn't like how his brother earned his living, perhaps? The thought made her uncomfortable.

The waiter delivered a basket filled with warm sourdough rolls and whipped butter, giving her a moment to regain her composure. She was letting her attraction to Jordan cloud her judgment, and it had to stop. After spending a few hours in his company, she discovered that not only was she attracted to him sexually, she actually liked him and found herself trying to justify his association with the agency. She'd never become the great investigative journalist she dreamed of if she didn't maintain her focus on the purpose of their association. He was a story. A means to an end. Nothing more. Sexual attraction be damned.

"Do you work for an architectural firm here in the city?" she asked, unwrapping the linen napkin covering the rolls and offering him one.

"Until a couple of months ago, I'd spent eight years with a firm in Los Angeles."

She sliced her roll and slathered it with butter. "What happened?"

A furrow of irritation crossed his face. "It's a long, boring story." He picked up his wineglass and took a sip, then turned his attention to the moonbeams reflecting on the ocean.

"Sounds interesting to me," she prompted, hoping he'd give her a glimpse into his past. For the sake of her story and *not* because she was interested in Jordan.

The low-toned conversation of the other patrons surrounded them, along with nondescript instrumental music flowing softly from the speakers. She looked at his hands, at his long, tapered fingers wrapped around the wineglass and imagined him sketching a high-rise, or maybe a child-care center. Her mother had always told her that long fingers were a sign of creativity. In this case, Mom was right again, she thought.

If he was truly an architect, she firmly reminded herself. This could be part of the role he was playing to swindle her out of money he believed she had. She couldn't afford to be swept away by the fantasy Jordan was creating. A fantasy she'd paid him to create.

He turned his attention back to her just as the waiter delivered their meal. As he'd promised, Jordan shared his order of giant stuffed mushroom caps by setting one on her bread plate.

She smiled her thanks and dug into the delectable seafood. "What happened in L.A.?" she asked.

"I started out at Lawrence and Brooks shortly after college," he began while adding salt and pepper to his dinner. "I worked during the day, and went to grad school at night. It took me a while to finally finish my education, but I'd been told that once I had my master's I'd be placed on the fast track."

She added dressing to her salad, then worked on cutting the larger lettuce into smaller pieces. "Sounds like you had a promising career ahead of you."

"I thought so," he said between bites of stuffed mushroom. "Once I finished my education and they promoted me to vice president, the partners talked about a senior vice presidency in my future. After a couple of years and my next promotion, they dangled a partnership carrot in front of me." He kept his voice well modulated, conveying a lack of emotion his eyes denied.

She paused over her salad. "I take it no partnership was forthcoming."

He shook his head, and reached for his wine. "No partnership," he said, the hardness of his eyes creeping into his voice.

"You're bitter," she said without thinking.

He set his fork aside and looked at her intently. "I suppose I am. How would you feel? I was lied to,

Cait. They used me. The bastards used my talent to design a multi-million-dollar high-rise development, then failed to deliver on their promise. If we won the bid for the development, I was told the partnership was mine. I worked for six months perfecting the presentation, won the bid and made the firm a hell of a lot of money, then the partnership was handed over to the nephew of one of the senior partners."

"Gee, where would we be without a little nepotism to ruin our plans?" she complained, and shook her head in disgust. "What'd you do?"

"I quit."

"Quit? After everything you'd accomplished, you just walked away?" No way could she walk away. Ever since she was a kid, she'd wanted to be a reporter. She couldn't imagine giving up something she'd worked so hard to achieve.

"I don't like being used."

Unexpected guilt swamped her. Was she really no better than the partners who'd lied to him? She was using him too for her own ends.

She felt like a slug.

A very low, slimy slug.

"I'm sorry," she said, not sure if she was apologizing for what had happened to him, or because of what she was doing to him herself. But what if he was using her? What if this was merely a fabrication to gain her sympathy so she'd hand money over by the fistful?

He let out a long breath. "No. I apologize. It's still an open wound."

Was it really? She had no way of knowing what was truth and what was part of the game he was playing with her. The lines were definitely becoming blurred and she needed time to sort out everything she'd learned so far. Discovering if he was truly an architect would be relatively simple, provided she asked the right questions. "So what are you doing now?"

"I've placed and won a few bids since coming home. It's a beginning. A slow one, but a beginning."

"You're going into business for yourself?" Interesting, she thought. Maybe that's why he'd agreed to be her valentine. Perhaps he wanted the money to help build his own firm. Not that it made swindling anyone right, but at least she understood his motivation, and perhaps the lengths to which he would go to achieve his own goal. And the information would go a long way to provide her with the added depth she wanted for her story.

A determined glint entered his eyes. "I'm not going to depend on someone else for my success. If I make it, I'll make it on my own," he said with a steely edge to his voice.

She shifted the conversation to his current projects, and listened with rapt attention, taking mental notes to retrieve later for her investigation, and trying with difficulty to ignore the guilt pricking her conscience. By the time they left the restaurant half an hour later, she'd learned the name of the developer of a bid he'd recently been awarded, something she could easily verify.

They strolled slowly along the wharf, pausing occasionally to peer into the windows of various shops and tourist traps. A chilled breeze blew across the boardwalk and Cait shivered.

"Cold?" Jordan asked.

She smiled up at him. "Just a chill. I'm fine."

A chill, or regret that she was using Jordan? she wondered. She tried to shake the guilt, but a little voice continued to niggle her conscience that perhaps he was exactly what he appeared to be—an architect trying to rebuild his career after a rough setback and filling in for his brother who was out of town. Perhaps her lead was mistaken, but she didn't quite believe that either. Jordan had taken the money she'd offered him and was with her now because she'd paid him. He might be charming, have the kind of body that made a girl think of all sorts of delicious ways to lure him into her bed, but he *was* technically her employee. He might have a killer grin that made her knees weak, except she'd hired him to be her valentine and he was delivering a service. She'd do well to remember that and forget about fantasies.

They reached the last of the shops and he steered her toward the end of the pier. The yellowed fog lights kept them from being surrounded by total darkness, but the intimacy of the setting, with the water lapping slowly against the pilings and the sounds drifting away behind them, wasn't lost on her. She braced her arms on the railing and looked out over the ocean. Breathing in the salty sting of sea air, she tried to forget that they were virtually alone.

He braced his elbow on the railing beside her. "Who are you, Cait Sullivan?" he asked, his voice low and loverlike.

She turned and met his gaze. Tension coiled inside her at the intensity shining in his eyes.

He's a story, she told herself. *This is all an act, an award-winning performance.*

"Just a girl with a fantasy," she whispered.

He watched her with such thoroughness, her breath caught. His gaze dropped and lingered at her breasts. Her nipples tightened and pressed against the raspy lace of her bra. She didn't even have to close her eyes to imagine his hands touching her.

He wrapped his finger around one of her curls. "I want to kiss you."

Her stomach tightened. "You do?"

He nodded and moved closer. "Yeah, I do," he said, sliding his hand deeper into her hair until he cupped the back of her neck with his large, warm hand.

She stood as still as a statue, unable to tear her gaze from his. Her breath stopped and she couldn't speak, couldn't move, and she wasn't sure she wanted to.

Slowly, he lowered his head and brushed his lips gently across hers, tentatively at first, then his tongue touched the seam of her lips. She opened her mouth and his tongue swept inside to tangle with hers, gently urging her to participate. He shifted, pulling her into his arms. His body was warm and hard, and the masculine scent of him wrapped around her and made her forget about stories and scandals and think only of him and the way he was turning her insides to Jell-O.

She slipped her arms inside his leather jacket and around his middle. Her breasts tingled and tightened, rubbing seductively against the lace of her bra. Arching against him, she reveled in the sheer pleasure of contact. When he slanted his mouth over hers to deepen the kiss, she moaned and lost herself in the wild sensations surging through her. He responded by pulling her even tighter, pressing her sensitized breasts against his firm, wide chest.

Sweet Mary, the man could kiss!

He massaged the back of her neck with one hand, the other trailing over her hip and up her side to cup her breast beneath her jacket. She shivered, and it had nothing to do with the cool sea breeze. It was more like a fever. Jordan had her burning up inside, melting.

The horn of a passing ship intruded, answered by the blare of the fog horn from the lighthouse in the distance. That's all they were, she thought as Jordan's hand skimmed under her sweater. Ships. Ships passing through each other's lives for entirely different purposes. And neither of them were honorable.

She eased away from him, her heart snagging as she felt the reluctance with which he let her go. She risked a glance at him, at the arousal burning in his eyes, and resisted the urge to step back into his arms and lift her lips to his for another bone-melting kiss. The wind tossed a lock of hair across his forehead. She itched to smooth it back in place, but suspected the contact would have her begging for more of his intoxicating kisses.

She shoved her hands into the side pockets of her jacket instead. "We should be going. It's getting late."

He removed her hands from her pockets and laced their fingers together. She met his gaze and was startled by his lazy smile and the gentle affection in his eyes. She waited for him to say something, but he dipped his head and brushed his mouth gently over hers. The spark of awareness continued to spiral through her long after he ended the brief kiss.

"You're an intriguing woman, Cait. And I'm looking forward to unlocking your mysteries."

Cait shivered again. He hadn't meant the gentle words as a threat, but she thought of them in that context just the same. If Jordan succeeded in discovering her mysteries, that'd be the end of her story.

The only problem was, she didn't know which would affect her more—the loss of her story...or the loss of Jordan.

4

"SULLIVAN!"

Cait stood and peered over the top of her cubicle. Her editor, Edmund Davidson, stood in the doorway to his office, hands jammed on his hips, glasses pushed high onto his creased forehead. His lips thinned into a tight line, and then he bellowed, "A minute, Sullivan!"

Cait groaned. Either he was going to blast her latest effort to breathe some life into the floral-show piece, or he'd somehow learned about her undercover sideline as an investigative reporter. Which was not impossible, she thought as she crossed the bullpen to Edmund's office, especially if Jen had ratted her out in an attempt to protect her from herself.

She ignored the fierce expression on Edmund's face and breezed past him into his office. Files and papers littered the desktop and covered the keyboard to his computer. A curl of steam rose from a mug of fresh coffee resting near the edge of the desk beside a framed studio photograph of his children and dozens of grandchildren.

"Have a seat," he said in his huge, booming voice as he closed the door.

Cait sat and waited while Edmund circled the desk and lowered his big, former pro-football body into the sturdy leather chair. Her boss blustered, a lot, but no one at the *Herald* could claim the former Chicago Bear defensive lineman was difficult to work for. The only thing he asked of his reporters was good reporting and loyalty, not only to the paper, but to him.

Something her nocturnal activities defied.

Considering she'd already established a believable cover, as well as made contact with the agency, if Edmund had somehow discovered what she was up to during her off-hours, the worst he would do was order her to shelve the story and she'd be out a couple of thousand bucks. He might even find the story viable and give it to one of the "boys," but not before he'd read her the riot act for daring to overstep her bounds, behind his back no less.

She didn't want to risk losing the story that had the potential of finally gaining her the respect she craved. If there was something going on at Fantasy for Hire that bore investigating, then she was determined to uncover the truth. Wasn't it her job to enlighten the unsuspecting public, if indeed the agency was everything Louden Avery claimed? If it turned out that Fantasy for Hire was legitimate, then no harm done.

After what she'd learned about her valentine the previous evening, she had a feeling Jordan McBride wouldn't exactly share her philosophy, no matter how noble her intentions. He'd been burned, lied to, and had made his thoughts on that matter more than clear. She was deceiving him, but if she was going to change her area of expertise from fluff to hard-hitting journalism, she didn't have a choice.

Or did she?

Edmund dropped her article on the flower show in

front of her. "What's the meaning of this?" he asked, not giving her time to wallow in guilt.

She leaned forward to get a better look. Angry slashes of red covered the crisp white paper. The darned thing looked as if someone had bled all over it.

Edmund's glasses dropped onto the bridge of his nose. He pulled them off and tossed them on the desk. "Your assignment was to report on the show."

"I did," she said. "But there—"

"Who, what, when, where and why, Sullivan," he interrupted. "No more. No less."

"But Paul Franklin is a major player in the financial district. He's recently contributed thousands of dollars to the presidential—"

Edmund pulled in a deep breath and let it out slowly, a sign he was struggling to hold back that monstrous bite. She'd seen his legendary temper flare at unsuspecting reporters who dared argue with him, and while she'd received her own share of Edmund's disapproval, she'd never openly defied him. Until lately.

"What does that have to do with his wife's garden society?" he demanded.

She sucked in her own calming breath. "Nothing," she admitted.

"Get rid of it, Sullivan."

"But I thought—"

"I'm not paying you to think! Your assignment was to tell your readers about the show. They don't give a rip about Paul Franklin and his political aspirations. They want to hear about the blue ribbons his wife's garden club won for their pretty posies. If they want to know what Franklin is up to, they'll read about it in the business section."

Frustration ran deep, but Cait bit her lip and stood. If the two years she'd been at the paper had taught her anything, it was that arguing with Edmund was a waste of time. He had it in his mind that she was a fluff reporter and that's all she'd ever be in his eyes.

So why was she even wasting her time with the Fantasy piece? Maybe because if Edmund didn't go for the story, another paper would. Maybe another more prestigious paper that would value her talent and applaud her initiative. A paper that would pay her to think.

"Is that all?" she asked, not because she was hoping to please him, but because it was expected.

He rifled through the papers scattered over his desk, then handed her a slip with a printed address. "The animal shelter you're covering that the San Francisco Kennel Club is sponsoring has added the Windsor Group to its list of contributors," he said. "Marilyn Windsor is hosting a formal ground-breaking ceremony Friday morning followed by a benefit brunch to raise money. San Francisco's society is coming out in droves to show their support for Marilyn Windsor's newest pet project. Cover it."

Cait took the paper from him and ignored his chuckle at his own pun. Another boring article covering the even more bored socialites of the San Francisco elite, she thought, turning to leave.

"And Sullivan?" he said as she reached for the door.

She glanced at him over her shoulder. He rubbed at

the tension knotting his neck, tension he no doubt blamed on her.

"Just tell me who's there and what they're wearing. This isn't a piece on animal rights."

"Yes, sir," she said and left the office.

One of these days, she'd show Edmund Davidson and the rest of the smug reporters covering "real" news at the paper that she, Cait Sullivan, had what it took to make it to the top. And if she had her way, that would be very, very soon.

"One of these days," she muttered, slipping back into her cubicle. She closed the file she'd been working on and pulled up the article on the flower show.

After another series of rewrites, she was finally able to put the flower piece to bed and still make deadline. By the time she left the paper for the day, her frustration level had soared to new heights, caused primarily by Edmund's inability to see her as anything more than a face pretty enough to cover the bored and wealthy events of the city.

A short while later, she pulled her fifteen-year-old hatchback into the sloped driveway of her brother's Pacific Heights home and cut the engine. Her old car had other ideas and continued to run for another two seconds. After a sputter, a spit and a final groaning shimmy, it quieted. Pulling her laptop from the passenger seat, she left the vehicle and hurried toward the brick steps leading up to the massive double doors, anxious for a hot bath and a night in front of the laptop, putting together the pieces of the Fantasy story.

She stopped dead.

Built-in lights cast a luminous glow over the steps

and she peered closer. A variety of flower petals littered the steps. "Camellias?" she murmured, slowly
following the trail of white and pink flora scattered
over the steep brick staircase. There wasn't a single
camellia bush within fifty feet of her brother's house.

"What on earth?" She bent and ran her fingers over
a handful of petals toward the brief ledge of the first
landing where the steps curved in the direction of the
house. Just what she needed, she thought sourly. After the terrible day she'd had, she was exhausted. The
last thing she wanted was to spend her evening cleaning up after some prankster.

Grumbling to herself, she climbed the remaining
steps to the front porch. She stopped again, staring in
disbelief.

Pots with flowers ready for outdoor planting,
vases, from crystal to brass, were filled with colorful
flower arrangements. Even a few hanging plants
lined the porch, resting against the base of the wide
stone retaining wall that served as a porch railing.
One filled with creeping Jenny hung from the door-
knob. She recognized coralbells, carnations of nearly
every color of the rainbow and heart-shaped cycla-
men. Pots of fragrant corkscrew flower and even clo-
ver rested on the wrought-iron settee beneath the bay
window. Baskets filled with chrysanthemums and
calla lily waited near the door. There was even a
small, indoor citrus tree.

No doubt the florist had made a mistake and delivered the flowers to her rather than the hotel for her
parents' anniversary party on Saturday, but she'd ordered yellow and white roses, her mother's favorites.
She didn't know anyone that would send her flowers,

let alone bombard her with such an overwhelming variety. Not only hadn't she had a steady boyfriend in ages, the last guy she'd dated for any length of time had made it clear he believed romance was nothing more than a feminine conspiracy designed to emasculate the male population.

She hefted her laptop case and purse higher onto her shoulder and carefully picked her way through the flowers and plants to snag the white envelope taped to the door. Opening the envelope, she slid a thin sheet of onion-skin paper from the covering and read the thick, masculine scrawl:

> Only the most beautiful things
> begin with the letter C.
> Your valentine

She read and reread the note from Jordan. Based on the generosity of his gift, he obviously didn't hold the idea of romance in a disparaging light. Quite the contrary, and she couldn't help feeling the weight of another guilt-filled brick on her shoulders.

"Stop it," she muttered, slipping her key into the lock. Jordan was a story. It wasn't as if he'd swept her off her feet or anything.

She stepped into the quiet of the large, rambling house, set her things on the antique rosewood table in the entry before beginning to haul Jordan's gift inside the house. After more than half a dozen trips, the elegant table in the formal dining room was overflowing with pots, vases and baskets. She knew she was being ridiculous, but by the time she'd brought all the flora into the house, she couldn't stop the feeling that if this had been a real budding romance, if she hadn't paid Jordan to be her valentine, his thoughtful and completely outrageous gesture would have completely swept her off her feet.

Who was she trying to kid? she chastised herself, setting the last of the red carnations on the glossy tabletop. Even though she realized she had paid him to be her valentine, he still managed to not only overwhelm her, but take her completely by surprise. Never had anyone done anything so completely thoughtful or so fantastically excessive. The ingenuity of his gift touched her deep inside, deep down in that place she'd always imagined reserved for tender feelings and emotions only that special someone was supposed to be able to reach.

She couldn't think about it. Or him. Not in those terms. Jordan McBride was a story. Nothing more, nothing less, she thought, borrowing Edmund Davidson's favorite line. Right now, she had steps to sweep before the rain started again or she'd be plucking petals from the brick by hand.

She grabbed a broom and dustpan, then headed toward the front door. Swinging the door open wide, she stepped onto the porch and nearly collided with her oldest sister, Linda.

"What are you doing here?" Cait asked.

"It's nice to see you, too, Cait." Linda gave a pointed look at the petals scattered over the porch. "What did you do? Blow up a flower shop?"

Being the youngest of five children, she'd grown accustomed to her sisters and oldest brother running interference in her life. She usually accepted their so-called concern in relatively good humor, but her current situation wasn't high on her list of items she was willing to share—yet. She didn't care to analyze the reasons behind that decision either. Some things were just better left alone, and right now, she had enough guilt to last her a lifetime without inviting Linda to add to it.

"No, I didn't blow up a flower shop." Cait laughed and stepped around her sister to begin sweeping the steps. Ignoring the curiosity brimming over in her sister's gaze, she concentrated instead on moving camellia petals from step to step into a small pile at the base.

"What *are* you doing here?" Cait asked when Linda came up behind her. "I thought you and John were going to be out of town until Saturday."

"He came down with a bug, so we had to come home early." Linda sat on the top step and grinned. "So you gonna tell me what's with all the flowers, or can I just assume you had a date with the FTD guy?"

Cait shrugged, just a quick jerk of one shoulder, because she couldn't come up with a plausible explanation...other than the truth.

"Caitie?"

Cait let out a puff of air that fluttered her bangs. There were moments when she wished she'd been born an only child. Right now was one of those moments.

Turning, she braced her hand on the top of the broom handle and looked up at her sister. "Someone sent me flowers, okay?"

"From this mess, it looks like he sent you an entire garden." Linda's laughter was genuine. "Is it a *special* someone?" she prompted, her grin widening.

Cait bit her lip, wondering how much she should tell her sister. The problem was, once she told Linda, Sharon and Donna would know about her "special someone," and before long, her very protective older brother, Brian, and she just wasn't ready to answer questions about Jordan.

What was wrong with her? The only thing special about Jordan was the story, why couldn't she remember that? He was a solution to her stalled career. Just because he'd shown her he had a romantic streak meant absolutely nothing. She'd *paid* him to be romantic, for crying out loud.

"You'll meet him Saturday" was all she was willing to admit. "I'm bringing him to Mom and Dad's anniversary party."

She finished sweeping the steps, then headed up to start on the porch.

"How long have you known him?" Linda asked, following her.

"Not long," she answered, keeping her attention on her task.

"How long is not long?"

"I met him three days ago."

"Three days and he's already sending you flowers?"

Cait straightened and faced her sister. "What's the big deal?" she asked, frowning. "It's just a few flowers. Why are you here anyway?"

Linda snapped her fingers and reached into her purse. "Sharon called me. She tried to get in touch with you, but said you forgot to turn on the answering machine again." She pulled a sheet of paper from her purse. "Since you're in charge of the caterer, you need to decide what you're going to do. They're having trouble with those stuffed grape leaves Dad likes and wanted to substitute them with crab rolls. Something about it being the wrong time of year for grapes?"

Cait took the paper with the caterer's number from her sister and stuffed it into the pocket of her black wool trousers. "I'll call them tomorrow. Is that the only reason you came over?"

"Are you trying to get rid of me? Is the FTD man coming for a visit?" Linda teased, her sea-green eyes filled with laughter.

Cait couldn't help the smile tugging her lips. "As if I could get rid of you," she complained. "And no. I don't have a date. Have you had dinner yet?"

"I took Mom shopping for a dress for the party and we had dinner downtown. But I'd love some tea."

"Tea, it is," she said and set the broom against the side of the house.

"Good grief, Cait!" Linda exclaimed once they entered the house. Her sister halted at the entrance to the dining room. "Either he's a) head over heels in love, b) you were really good, or c) he's hoping you're going to be really good."

Cait rolled her eyes. "It's d) none of the above," she countered, stepping into the kitchen. "He's just trying to make an impression."

"It's working." Linda slipped onto the white leather bar stool at the breakfast bar. "I'm impressed. That must have cost him a fortune."

I paid him a fortune, Cait thought.

"I wonder where he found crocus this time of year?

You know that's nearly impossible to find in February, don't you?"

"I wouldn't know," Cait said, filling the teapot with tap water.

Linda propped her elbows on the white ceramic tiles of the bar and rested her chin in her hands. "He must be rich," she said, flipping a chestnut curl behind her ear.

Yeah, from milking innocent women out of their fortunes.

"I guess," Cait said, pulling a pair of china cups from the cabinet.

Her sister talked about the variety of flowers, but Cait's mind wandered. What if it wasn't true? What if Louden Avery had lied? What if Jordan wasn't part of some scam, but was everything he claimed: a self-employed architect filling in for his out-of-town brother?

Evidence to the contrary lay on the dining-room table, she reminded herself, absently nodding in agreement to something Linda said. Sending flowers was a romantic gesture, sure, but not to the extent Jordan had gone. He believed she was rich, a target, and he was merely following standard operating procedure in an attempt to weasel her out of her supposed fortune. Just because he'd kissed her as though he meant it was immaterial. His bone-melting kisses, the flowers that all started with the initials of her first name, even the chocolates in the big, red velvet box were all part of the game he was so expertly playing with her. A game in which he hoped to be the winner...of a fortune she didn't possess.

It took a little maneuvering, but she effectively

managed to change the subject from Jordan to her parents' anniversary party. They spent the next hour working out a few of the last-minute details that tend to crop up when planning such a large-scale affair. Afterward, she showed Linda to the door with a promise to let her know if Brian called with a change of plans. The last they'd heard, their brother was deep in negotiations with a Japanese supplier for a component for his computer company, Sullivan Systems, and he didn't think he'd be able to wrap things up in time to make it back for the party.

With a final promise to handle the caterer, and to meet her sisters for lunch at the hotel on the day of the party, Cait finally had the remainder of the evening to herself. The hot bath she'd been craving since she'd left the office beckoned, so she retrieved the cordless phone, in case one of her sisters called, and headed upstairs.

Ten minutes later, she rested her head against the back of the sunken tub and closed her eyes. The heated, lilac-scented water lapped luxuriously against her skin and slowly began to ease the tension from her body. Images of Jordan filtered through her mind. She saw his dark head as he leaned forward, the intensity of his hazel eyes as he lowered his lips to a mere breath away, felt his hand against her hip, his long, lean fingers brushing against the waistband of her jeans...until the phone rang, dousing the erotic images.

She wiped her hand on the thick, fluffy towel, then reached for the cordless. "Hello," she said in a not-so-inviting voice.

"Am I interrupting something?"

She sat up straight and nearly dropped the phone at the sound of Jordan's deep, masculine voice. "Uh, no. I was just—"

"Is that water?"

She eased back down into the tub. *Seduction.* Wasn't she supposed to be seducing him?

"As a matter of fact, it is," she said, using the sultriest voice she could muster. "You caught me taking a bubble bath."

A loud crash sounded through the receiver. "Jordan? Jordan, are you okay?"

More crackling sounds, followed by a muffled curse. "Sorry," Jordan said after a moment. "Phone slipped."

A satisfied grin tugged her lips. "Thank you for the flowers. I can't remember the last time anyone tried so hard to please me," she said, letting her words drip with innuendo.

He cleared his throat and her grin widened.

"I'm glad you're enjoying them."

"Was there something in particular *you* wanted?" she asked deliberately. She could think of a few things she wanted. And a tall, handsome, hazel-eyed architect topped her list.

"Do you have plans for tomorrow night?"

Even if she did have other plans, she'd cancel them in a heartbeat if it meant she'd be that much closer to exposing Fantasy for Hire. "I'm all yours," she practically purred in the name of professional journalists everywhere. "Did you have something special in mind?"

He chuckled, the sound as teasing as a gentle caress. "I'll do everything in my power to see that you're pleased. Good night, Cait," he said and then he was gone.

She set the phone on the ledge, sank lower into the warmth of the water and blew out a stream of breath. Jordan McBride had the power to do more than please, she thought, wondering how he'd managed to turn the tables on her so effectively. He had the power to set her soul on fire.

And there was nothing professional about it.

5

Tall, dark and gorgeous! For a price, anyone can have their own personal boy-toy. Looking for a lusty bachelor to fulfill your most erotic fantasy? *Fantasy for Hire* has them. But a word of warning before handing over the plastic, ladies. Take care to hide the trust fund, because these walking, talking dreams come true are looking to fulfill their own fantasies at your expense.

CAIT LEANED BACK and reread the paragraph, smiling to herself. Even if she had zilch for verification of Avery's allegations against Jordan and his brother, Austin, at least the first draft of her article was beginning to take shape.

She traced her finger along the pink petal of a carnation that stood in a vase atop the Queen Anne desk in the den. Unless how Jordan made her knees go weak and her heart beat triple time counted as proof of Fantasy for Hire's illicit activities, she was in big trouble. She hadn't one iota of solid evidence, other than a major dent in her savings account. She had to come up with more than a kiss she'd never forget, or enough flora to open her own flower shop. Otherwise, her article would never materialize, and her career would never get that crucial jump start that would catapult her into serious journalism.

She drummed her acrylic nails on the gleaming desktop and glanced at the clock. Jordan would be arriving any moment now. For what, she hadn't a clue, which did nothing to quell the flutter of anticipation in her stomach. Considering he'd already gone crazy in the gift department, she should probably be a little worried about what was next on his agenda.

She blew out a stream of breath and shut down the computer. She couldn't afford to be worried. If she didn't let Jordan know in no uncertain terms she was more than ready, willing and able for "the works" tonight, she'd never get the verification she needed for her story.

Just as she slipped the last file with her notes into the top drawer of the desk, the doorbell chimed. She slammed the drawer shut and headed toward the double doors, adjusting her skirt, tucking in her blouse and fluffing her bangs. With a deep, fortifying breath, she pasted what she hoped was a sultry, inviting grin on her face and opened the door.

Her breath stilled and her heart beat a heavy rhythm in her chest at the sight of Jordan's heart-stopping grin and the wicked sparkle in his gaze. His eyes swept down the length of her, and she felt each stroke of his gaze as if he'd caressed her. When he finished his perusal and met her eyes again, it was with a look that held not only interest, but a heated, sensual gleam that had her body and mind humming with forbidden anticipation.

Only supreme concentration enabled her to dispel the erotic images filtering through her mind. She had to stop this nonsense. Getting lost in the fantasy wasn't her goal even if she *had* paid him to be her own personal dream come true.

She propped her shoulder against the stucco wall, crossed her feet at the ankles and attempted an amused expression. Her gaze fell on the huge, gaily wrapped wicker basket in his arms. "Is that a basket in your hands or are you just happy to see me?" she quipped in her best Mae West voice, giving her curls a pat.

His answering chuckle warmed her clear to her toes. "Both," he said, stepping into the foyer. He held the basket up for her inspection. "I brought you something to make your evening more enjoyable."

She peered into the basket. An array of scented candles in small red and white glass votive holders, along with perfumed bubble bath from her favorite specialty shop, were nestled inside. Champagne, a single, elegantly carved crystal champagne flute, a square wrapped box from an exclusive lingerie shop, and a bowl filled with out-of-season strawberries completed the latest offering. The makings of a perfect romantic evening, except for that very telling single champagne flute.

Let him know you're ready, willing and able, she thought.

She smiled up at Jordan. "Looks like a winning beginning to me." Using her foot, she pushed the door closed. "But we'll need another glass."

That got his attention. He set the basket on the antique table in the entryway and turned to face her, a light frown pulling his eyebrows together. "Another glass?"

Slowly, she straightened and advanced toward him. Keeping her gaze locked with his, she lifted her hand and traced a lazy pattern around the center button of his cotton dress shirt. "You were planning to join me, weren't you?"

He stretched his neck slightly, as if his paisley necktie had suddenly tightened. "Join you?"

"Hmm," she murmured, moving closer still. She flattened her palm against his firm, wide chest, then eased her hand upward to tug on the knot of his tie, bringing his lips closer to hers. "The tub *is* large enough for two," she whispered, then lightly brushed her mouth against his.

A shock wave of heat raced through her the moment her lips touched his, startling her. She looked into his hazel eyes, at the gold flecks practically flaring with heat, and before she could think about consequences or stories or anything more important than kissing Jordan, she slipped her hand around his neck and urged him closer.

His arm banded her waist, pulling her flush against him. The tips of her already sensitized breasts brushed against his chest. The flutters in her abdomen fanned the low, simmering heat, spreading it outward to her limbs. She breathed in his scent, that special blend of aftershave and Jordan.

He dipped his head and nuzzled the sensitive spot behind her ear. "What are you doing to me, Cait?"

She couldn't answer him. How could she be expected to form a coherent thought when her body was alive with anticipation? Instead, she applied a slight bit of pressure to the back of his neck and demanded, "Just kiss me, Jordan. Kiss me now."

He pulled back and looked down at her. His answering grin was devilish enough to make her toes curl into the soft leather of her black pumps. His lips capturing hers was enough to make her moan softly, wreathe her arms around his neck and press even closer, lining her body with his.

When the wool of his trousers rasped against her nylon-clad legs, all she could think about was the possibility of feeling those firm, muscular thighs against her slimmer ones unencumbered by clothing. His tongue teased hers in a mating game that made her feel hot and tight and more aroused than she'd ever imagined possible.

When his hand settled on her hip and rocked her closer still, there was no doubt left in her mind that Jordan wanted her as much as she wanted him.

Or that he wants the fortune he thinks you have.

What fortune? she snapped at the voice of reason inside her that sounded suspiciously like Jen. Fluff journalism wasn't exactly on the top-ten list of high-paying professions.

You're paying him to do this to you.

Money well spent, she argued, then sifted her fingers through the strands of sable hair at his collar.

Do you really want to do this?

She sighed and stepped reluctantly out of Jordan's warm embrace. Yes, she wanted him, more than she'd ever wanted another man in her entire life. And if he'd asked her five seconds ago, she would have eagerly led the way to the bedroom and made love to him. There was a scandal just waiting for her to bust wide open, and climbing into the sack with Jordan, no matter how tempting, would destroy her chances of exposing it. Her goal was to get him to proposition her for money, and so far, all he'd done was set her soul on fire without so much as asking for a receipt.

If she wanted to be a "real" reporter, then she'd better start doing some "real" investigating. Now. Because in three days, the contract for her valentine fantasy would expire.

"I'll get that extra glass," she said, not surprised by the shakiness in her voice. "Why don't you go on upstairs? It's the last room on the right with an adjoining bath. I'll be right there."

His hand on her arm stopped her. "Cait, what do you think is going to happen here tonight?" he asked, his tone as cautious as the look in his eyes.

He wasn't supposed to be cautious. He was supposed to jump at the chance to seduce her. If his intent was to seduce her out of her money, then why wasn't he racing her to the bedroom?

"Nothing," she said and smiled despite the doubts clouding her mind, "except the pleasant evening you promised me."

He let her go and she hurried into the dining room to the cabinet filled with elegant china, crystal stemware and silver serving pieces. Her hand shook when she reached inside for the flute, and she ordered herself to calm down. The fact that Jordan's kisses turned her inside out with need meant nothing. He was a scoop, and while she was pretty darned certain she had the seduction angle of it down to a near science, she needed to find a way to get him to ask her for more money. A lot more money than what she'd already paid him because considering the gifts he'd been giving her all week, the two thousand dollars could easily be considered a reasonable payment for the services he'd provided as her hired valentine.

She closed the etched-glass door of the china cabinet and headed toward the stairs. The sound of running water greeted her as she climbed the curved staircase to the upper floor. Brian's elegant home hadn't done the trick. She needed something, some vital key that would push Jordan to reveal the real purpose behind Fantasy for Hire.

Something that didn't include tangled sheets and the promise of pleasure beyond her wildest imaginings.

And something that didn't include her falling for Jordan McBride.

JORDAN STOPPED in the doorway. Staring at the huge, king-size bed, he knew firsthand the true meaning of temptation. He released an aggravated breath, shoved aside the wicked, erotic fantasies slamming into him, and dropped the red, foil-wrapped package from the lingerie shop on the corner of the bed. Purposely, he headed into the adjoining bathroom as Cait had instructed.

Desire balled in his gut and burned hot. He wanted Cait, and he didn't doubt for a moment she wasn't equally interested, but until the contractual obligation as her valentine fantasy was fulfilled, there'd be no exploration of a serious relationship. Until then, no matter how much he wanted her, Cait Sullivan was off-limits, because when he made love to her, he wanted their coming together to stem from mutual affection and attraction, and not payment for services rendered.

He set the basket on the plush carpeting and adjusted the taps. What the hell was wrong with him? He had a beautiful woman practically begging him to make love to her, and what was he doing? Acting like a damned, noble fool when he wanted nothing more than to take what she was so blatantly offering.

He had half a mind to let his stupid moral code of honor slip down the drain with the water running in the tub. There was only so much a man could take, and Cait pressing her delectable little body against his had just about pushed him to the limit.

God, he couldn't remember the last time a woman had him so tied up in knots. He was finally beginning to understand why Austin had been such a bear during his courtship with Teddy. If his little brother had been feeling anything close to what he was suffering, then Austin had his belated sympathies.

He tested the water. Satisfied with the temperature, he lowered the level on the stopper to fill the tub, then poured the perfumed bubble bath into the water until the scent of vanilla rose with the steam from the water. Keeping his eye on the rising water level, he lit each of the two-and-a-half dozen vanilla and misty sea rose–scented candles. Then he set them out along the long marble vanity and the raised, tiled platform circling the back of the bathtub. He noted that it was, indeed, large enough for two.

After turning off the taps, he set the champagne flute on the marble vanity, then retrieved the sparkling wine from the basket. He worked the foil wrapper and aluminum wires to ease the cork loose.

"I take it this was for me."

Jordan turned at the honeyed purr of Cait's voice.

Desire rolled through him at the sweet, sensual sight of her wearing nothing but the white satin robe he'd brought her and an I'm-ready-for-some-serious-sin smile.

She flicked off the overhead light.

The cork to the champagne popped...prematurely.

The frothy liquid erupted over the side of the bottle, startling him. She laughed, a light, throaty sound, and tossed him a thick, fluffy hand towel.

"Sorry 'bout that," he muttered, feeling more embarrassed than the situation warranted.

She stepped farther into the warm, candlelit glow of the bathroom. White satin molded to the gentle curve of her hips and outlined her full breasts. The soft material reached midthigh, giving him more than a glimpse of her shapely legs. He may have been hired to fulfill her fantasy, but she definitely sparked a few fantasies in his mind.

"Will you join me?" she asked, brushing up beside him.

"Cait, I really don't think—"

Her grin widened as she held out a crystal flute. "I meant for a glass of champagne."

Denying a beautiful woman, especially one as tempting as Cait, was proving to be the toughest challenge he'd ever faced.

He took the flute from her and concentrated on filling the glasses. A whisper of sound caught his attention, followed by the sound of water sloshing in the enormous bathtub. He turned to find a pool of white satin lying on the floor, then caught a brief glimpse of a very feminine backside disappearing into the steamy, scented bath.

Blowing out a stream of breath, he shoved a hand through his hair, trying to figure out why he suddenly felt like a teenager about to experience his first romantic encounter.

Cait shifted, the bubbles of her bath preventing him from viewing anything more enticing than the barest hint of the gentle slope of her breasts. Clearing his throat, he reached into the basket, withdrew the cut-glass bowl filled with strawberries and set them on the edge of the tub before handing her a glass of champagne.

She smiled and lifted the glass toward him. "To fantasies," she said.

He crouched on the carpeting beside the tub. "To fantasies."

He watched her over the rim of his glass, amazed again by the interesting mix of contradictions she represented. The seductress, while exciting, fell short of overpowering the wholesomeness that constantly surrounded her. Even sitting in a tubful of perfumed bubbles, sipping expensive champagne and sinking her teeth into a plump strawberry, there was a down-to-earth quality about her that intrigued him. She was a mystery, and one he wouldn't mind discovering inch by slow, tortuous inch.

Her tongue innocently darted out and lapped at a rivulet of strawberry juice on the tip of her finger, sending a flash of heat firing through his veins. A grin tugged her lips, not the wicked grin of seductive promise, but one that filled her gaze with laughter.

She set her glass on the ledge, the laughter in her eyes shifting to concern. "You're frowning."

He set his own glass aside, then unbuttoned the

cuffs on his dress shirt to roll back the sleeves. "Who are you, Cait?" he asked, loosening the knot of his tie. *Besides the woman driving me crazy.*

Thanks to the bubble bath, he heard, more than saw, her pull her legs up to her chest. She leaned forward, bracing her arms on her upturned knees. "A client."

The sight of all that exposed flesh had him shifting closer to the tub. Droplets of water moistened her skin, an enticing golden color remaining from a summer tan that was enhanced by the soft glow of candlelight. The urge to touch, to smooth his hands over the contours of her skin proved too much to resist. Giving in to the need to touch her, he snagged the pink body sponge resting on the ledge and dipped it into the scented bath. "I'm not talking about our... professional relationship," he offered for lack of a better description.

He repeated the process, this time smoothing the sponge over her back, allowing the tips of his fingers to brush along her skin. She stiffened in a telling way—regardless of her blatant come-on about joining her in the tub, she was more show than go. It was something he found fascinating, endearing and curious all at the same time. "Aside from that," he said, continuing his ministrations. "Who are you really? I can't figure you out."

She closed her eyes and dropped her head against her slender forearms. "Just a girl with a fantasy," she said, the husky, sultry voice filled with caution.

The caution snagged his attention. "I want to know all about you, Cait. Tell me," he prompted, smoothing the soap-filled sponge along the length of her back. He was playing with fire, being this close to all that feminine allure. All he could think about was lifting her out of the tub and carrying her into the bedroom where they could make use of that king-size bed and embark on an intimate exploration of each other's bodies.

Her eyes snapped open, and she regarded him quizzically. "Not much to tell, really," she answered, straightening.

"Where'd you grow up?" he asked, dipping the sponge then smoothing it over her back again.

"Here, in San Francisco."

"What'd you study in college?"

Cait leaned forward, away from his very distracting touch. Warning bells loud enough to signal a nuclear attack went off in her head. "Jordan, what's this all about?" she asked. Had she blown her cover by coming on too strong? If he was suspicious of her motives for engaging his services, she'd have no story and no chance of recouping the cash she'd laid out for this little side venture.

He shrugged, then dropped the sponge in the water before settling back beside the tub. "I just want to get to know you better."

She regarded him carefully. He didn't look suspicious. In fact, he looked completely relaxed, while she was strung tighter than a bow aimed at a target. She reached for the glass and drained the last of the champagne, hoping to quell the uneasiness gathering in her stomach.

"There's not much to know," she said carefully. "An uneventful but happy childhood, even if I am the youngest of five kids. My brother, Brian, is the oldest, then there's Linda, Donna and Sharon, who all think my business is their business. Typical family stuff."

He refilled her glass. "What you see is what you get, huh?"

"Something like that," she murmured, despising the lie. Somewhere between the bone-melting kiss in the foyer and sitting naked in a bathtub while Jordan washed her back, she'd had the crazy notion that if she'd met him under normal circumstances, Jordan McBride could definitely be the kind of man she would have easily fallen in love with. Except there was nothing normal about their circumstances. And he was a scoundrel out to bilk her of her make-believe trust fund. Not exactly fairy-tale material, even if she was fully, femininely aware of him.

"This is my fantasy," she said, then took another sip of champagne. "I'd rather talk about you. How's the architectural business? Build any skyscrapers lately?"

A furrow of irritation crossed his face, but it disappeared so quickly, she wondered if her overactive imagination hadn't conjured the emotion.

"Actually," he said, resting his arms on the side of the tub, "I have a presentation tomorrow for a series of strip malls in a dozen cities from here down to Pismo."

His fingers absently flicked the bubbles, popping them.

Her stomach fluttered as another few square inches of concealing bubbles disappeared. "Sounds promising," she managed to say.

He shrugged. "Let's hope they like my designs. I

could use the money. I have office space to rent, equipment to buy and an assistant to hire. A commission like that will go a long way to helping me get established."

A staggering excitement shot through her. Finally, the mention of money. He needed cash, and maybe his reasons *were* legitimate, but his morally bankrupt methods were at issue. "What happens if you don't get that commission?" she asked, fighting to keep the excitement out of her voice.

"Something will come along," he said, the corner of his mouth lifting into the grin of a scoundrel as he popped another few square inches of the bubbles shielding her from his gaze. "It usually does."

She just bet it did, she thought, amazed by his flawless recovery.

"This is a pretty serious conversation for a fantasy," he said, leaning closer. The musky, masculine scent she'd come to associate with him mingled with the rich vanilla of the perfumed bath and teased her senses, sending off sparks of awareness and igniting images of something other than their scents tangling together.

She shrugged a slim shoulder in what she hoped was an unaffected gesture. Too bad her insides weren't unaffected. "I hadn't really thought about it. Besides, it's my fantasy."

He lifted his hand and trailed his knuckles gently along her cheek. "Tell me your fantasy, Cait." The husky undertone to his deep, velvet voice sent a warm little shiver down her spine. "What do you want?"

"For you to kiss me," she said before she had time

to think about what she was really doing. His gaze dipped to her mouth, and her lips parted involuntarily in invitation. Her breathing deepened as she leaned closer to the edge, closer to Jordan and the heavenly sensations she knew awaited her the moment their lips touched.

She slicked her tongue over her bottom lip, and his gaze heated. The promise of pleasure too much to resist, she reached up and wrapped the length of his tie around her wet hand to pull him close until their breaths mingled. "I want you to kiss me, Jordan," she repeated.

"It's your fantasy," he whispered, causing her pulse to tumble and career out of control the instant his lips pressed seductively against hers.

Her response frightened her as much as it thrilled her. How could she want someone like Jordan, someone morally bankrupt enough to swindle women out of money? She wasn't naive; she didn't believe for a moment she could be the one to make him change his wicked ways. But if he asked right now, if she had a fortune, she would have gladly handed it over if it meant the delicious sensations rippling through her body would never end.

One hand cupped her neck, his fingers sliding into her steam-dampened hair, the other dipped beneath the surface of the water, his fingertips lightly brushing against her rib cage. Her head spun, her mind whirled around images and sensations as he cajoled her tongue to mate with his in a kiss hotter and more erotic than anything she'd ever experienced. A moan caught in her throat when he palmed her breast in the warmth of his large hand. Heat, fierce and blazing, built inside her as his thumb lightly teased her nipple into a taut peak.

She despised that the sensual magic sparking between them was based on lies. She disliked it that he was still fully clothed.

She hated it when he ended the kiss!

"We can't do this, Cait." He stood and crossed to the hook where he'd hung his well-worn leather bomber jacket, leaving her wanting him and needing so much more than a tongue-tangling kiss to squelch the flames he fanned so effortlessly.

Why? she wanted to screech at him when he turned back to face her. Instead, she managed a saucy grin. "This isn't exactly how I envisioned my fantasy ending," she said with more sass than she was feeling.

"This isn't the end, sweetheart. It's just the beginning." He shrugged into his jacket and graced her with a grin guaranteed to speed up her pulse. "You might want to add a few more bubbles to your bath," he said, then disappeared through the door.

Cait looked down and gasped, grateful for the slightly murky cast to the water from all those popped bubbles, but judging by that grin he'd given her, he'd obviously seen plenty.

Ten minutes later, she plopped down on the middle of the bed. Her knees still felt weak from her encounter with Jordan, and she didn't think the humming in her body would ever quit. Jordan McBride was a tease of the worst kind!

Frustrated, she dialed Jen's number and waited for her friend to pick up the line.

"What are you doing?" she asked when Jen finally answered.

"In the middle of hot, sweaty jungle sex, why do you ask?" Jen quipped sarcastically.

She rolled her eyes in exasperation. "I need your help."

"With the boy-toy?"

"Yes. And bring ice cream."

"Sounds serious."

Cait slipped off the bed and walked to the bathroom with the cordless phone in her hand. The scented candles still burned in the red and white votive holders, the rich vanilla scent reminding her of what she wanted but had been withheld for reasons she didn't understand. "Very serious," she told Jen.

"I'll be there in about half an hour," Jen said. "Any special flavor?"

She lifted a votive candle from the ledge and blew out the flame. A curl of smoke wafted around her and she frowned. "Anything but vanilla."

6

CAIT DROPPED her spoon in the half-empty carton of Chunky Monkey ice cream. "This isn't working," she complained.

Jen wagged her spoon at Cait like a parent reprimanding a child. "Drowning your sorrows in ice cream rarely works. It just makes the disappointment a little easier to swallow."

Cait shook her head. "I'm not talking comfort food," she said, pulling her legs up to her chest. "I mean with Jordan. There has to be a story there. I can feel it."

"What you're feeling, my little friend, is lust," Jen teased, then slipped a mouthful of New York Super Fudge off her spoon.

Cait rolled her eyes in exasperation. "Would you please be serious?"

Jen gave her a knowing look. "I am being serious."

Cait let out a long-suffering breath, then balanced the carton of ice cream on her upraised knees. Jordan had awakened something hot and primitive inside her, she couldn't deny the truth, nor did she want to, but that didn't mean she was willing to shelve her chance to prove herself as a serious journalist for a few hours of what she suspected would be the most fulfilling, mind-blowing sex of her adult life.

"I felt it tonight," she said, tapping the edge of the carton. "I was so close I could almost touch it."

Jen lifted an arched eyebrow and grinned.

"To the truth." Cait laughed, then grasped the carton of comfort food. She wished the chilled container had the power to cool the heat that still simmered in her body from the last breath-stealing kiss they'd shared. "He mentioned needing money tonight to start his own business."

Jen shrugged. "So, you already knew he was a self-employed architect."

Cait dipped her spoon into the ice cream. "He *says* he's an architect. I'm still waiting for verification from the accreditation agency." She looked at her friend. "I need to get him to proposition me. For money."

"What have you told him about this trust fund of yours?" Jen asked, scraping the side of the carton.

"Nothing," Cait said, dropping her head against the thick butter-yellow cushion of the sofa, "other than it exists." Patience had never been one of her finer character traits, and she couldn't help wondering if she was just a little too anxious to prove or disprove Jordan's career claims. If he hadn't mentioned money tonight, she might have been willing to believe he was simply filling in for his out-of-town brother, that he had indeed relocated from Los Angeles to the Bay Area for all the legitimate reasons he'd stated. But, if he was planning to open his own architectural firm, then he'd need money, and a lot of it.

Cait lifted her head and grinned at Jen. "That's it! You're an absolute genius."

Jen frowned and her gaze filled with caution. "What'd I say?"

Setting the uneaten portion of her carton of Chunky Monkey on the cocktail table, Cait leaned forward, crossing her legs. "That's how I can get Jordan to proposition me."

"How?"

"If he *sees* the trust fund, if he can actually see for himself how much I'm worth, then any doubts he might have as to my value as a target will disappear. He'll be so consumed with greed, he won't have any choice but to ask me for the money." The only snag in her plan was that she was having a difficult time attributing greed to Jordan McBride.

Jen scooped up the last of her ice cream. "Just because he thinks you have money doesn't mean he's going to ask you for it. Didn't you say the agency was exchanging sex for money? Look at this place," Jen said, sweeping her arms wide. "It's hardly a ruin, and Mr. Valentine hasn't swept you off your feet and carried you away for a night of hot jungle sex yet."

"What if he hasn't because he isn't certain I have the kind of money he needs?" Excitement rippled through her, confident she'd finally discovered the vital key she'd been needing to unlock Jordan's deceit.

"There's one little problem with your grand plan to have Jordan unearth your trust fund, Cait. You don't have one."

Cait stood, her grin never faltering. "No," she said confidently, "but my brilliant, computer-guru brother has more high-tech equipment than anyone I know. And lucky for me, my best friend is *very* user-friendly."

The frown pulling Jen's finely arched eyebrows deepened. "I'm not following you," she said, setting the empty ice-cream container aside.

Cait tugged Jen's hand, pulling her to her feet. "We, my computer-geek pal," she said, guiding the other woman reluctantly down the corridor to Brian's home office, "are going to create the Cait Sullivan Trust. In fact, we're going to fictionalize an entire financial portfolio."

"We are?" Jen asked, peering around Cait to Brian's computer equipment.

Knowing her friend's obsession with high-tech equipment, Cait urged her toward the computers. "Yes, we are."

Jen dropped into the chair in front of the largest of the computer monitors, her eyes filled with anticipation. The custom, modular desk unit lined two full walls of her brother's home office, the equipment covering most of the space. "What if the hired hunk doesn't fall for it?" Jen asked, booting up the main hard drive.

Cait opened a drawer of the lateral file cabinet and walked her fingers across the files. A stab of guilt pricked her as she slid Brian's personal financial records from the cabinet. She added a folder labeled Investments to the others in her hand, then slipped another four with the names of various banking institutions from the cabinet. She peered into one of the bank files and swallowed a surprised gasp. Brian had made his fortune—literally, from the sizable amount indicated on the bank statement—in the computer business with the development of a new high-speed microprocessor chip, and while she knew he had money, she'd never cared about the particulars. Money was obviously not a problem, but at least now she understood Brian's insistence on paying for her parents' anniversary party, even if he couldn't attend.

"He'll have no choice," Cait said, closing the file drawer. "When we're through, Jordan McBride will be salivating at the thought of getting his hands on all those zeros."

THREE HOURS LATER, Cait lifted the last of the dummy documents from the color laser printer. Thanks to Jen's creative genius, they'd developed a financial portfolio impressive enough to have Donald Trump asking for her phone number.

Jen stretched her arms over her head and glanced at the wall clock. "Are you sure this isn't illegal or something?"

Cait laughed and tapped her nail against one of the doctored bank statements. "Only if I tried to use all this money I don't have," she quipped. "Prison orange would clash with my hair, don't you think?"

"I'm beginning to think white is more your color," Jen said, closing down the equipment.

Cait shook her head at the unsettling images floating through her mind. "As in bridal white?" she asked carefully.

Jen handed her another file and stood. "No. I was thinking more along the lines of straitjacket white."

Cait ignored that comment, gathered the last of the files, and ushered Jen out of the room. She wasn't crazy, even if those bridal-white images oddly mingled with thoughts of Jordan as she walked Jen to the front door.

Jen pulled her coat from the closet. "When do you plan on springing your newfound fortune on the hired hunk?"

"Tomorrow night," Cait said, stuffing her hands into the back pockets of her jeans. "I'm going to call him and ask him on a good, old-fashioned date of a movie and meal."

"And you plan on...what?" Jen asked, her voice laced with sarcasm. "Serving up your phony finances with dessert?"

"No. I'll be running late. He'll wait in the den, and a couple of those folders will be open on the coffee table where he can't miss them."

"And if he's late?" Jen asked, shrugging into her wool-blend coat.

"He won't be," Cait assured her, crossing the foyer to the door. "If I tell Jordan seven, he'll be ringing the doorbell at six fifty-nine."

Jen reached for the door and stopped. Looking over her shoulder, her eyes filled with concern. "Have you thought about what's going to happen when he finds out the truth?" Jen asked, the concern transferring to her voice.

"That I'm not rich?"

"No," Jen said, facing her, "that you've been lying to him. I'm getting the impression you really like this guy, Cait. And from what you've told me so far, there isn't much by way of overwhelming evidence that there's anything disreputable, or even sleazy, about Fantasy for Hire."

"That's what I'm trying to prove," Cait said quietly, confused by the fragment of hope that Jordan really was everything he claimed. On the surface, she knew he was just a story, no matter how important or career making. But deep down, she wanted all those bone-melting kisses to hold greater meaning.

What was wrong with her? The warmth that cascaded through her, or the need and desire that had such a hold on her wasn't any more real than the intensity of Jordan's gaze or the reverence of his touch. They were playing a game, only he had no idea she knew his strategy as well as her own. The kisses and the touches they'd shared were as fictitious as a fairy tale.

She was turning out to be a much more adept liar than she thought, she realized.

Jen slipped her purse over her shoulder and sighed. "Ever hear of the constitutional right about being innocent until proven guilty?" she asked.

"This isn't a court of law."

"Cait. You could be making a huge mistake. What if this guy is everything he says he is? What if he really is trying to set up his own business in San Francisco? He could very honestly be filling in for his brother who's out of town."

Cait pulled her hands from her pockets and wrapped them around her middle. "What are you saying?" she asked, but she knew the answer. If she was wrong, the money and work she'd put into exposing the agency would be nothing more than wasted effort. But, even worse, if Jordan truly did care about her, once he learned she'd been lying to him and using him to advance her career, he'd be angry and hurt. He'd been lied to and used once. He wouldn't take too kindly to learning that she'd done the same.

"I'm just saying that if you're wrong, this guy might not be very forgiving."

"If I'm wrong, then it's my problem," she said, unwilling to discuss her guilt with Jen. "So, I'll be out a little cash. It's not the end of the world."

Jen opened the door and stepped onto the porch. "You could be out more than cash, kiddo. You might lose your own little piece of the fairy tale."

Jen turned and hurried down the steps. Cait waited under the glow of the porch light until Jen's car pulled out of the sloped driveway before slipping back into the quiet of the large, rambling house with her best friend's words of warning ringing in her ears.

AN HOUR BEFORE SUNSET, Jordan pulled his four-wheel-drive truck into the driveway next to Austin's car and cut the engine. The presentation for the developer on the strip malls had gone longer than planned, and much better than expected. Even if he hadn't come home with a firm commitment tucked inside his briefcase, he still felt confident he'd be receiving a call before the end of the month, if not sooner.

Soon, Advanced Architectural Designs would become a reality. Maybe he'd even be able to sweet-talk his new senior graphics designer sister-in-law to create his firm's logo, he thought with a grin as he slid from the vehicle.

His firm. Two sweeter words he'd never heard.

Never again would he have to depend on another person as a yardstick to measure his own success, or his own happiness. Successes, and failures, would be his own. The projects he took on would be of his choosing, and not offered on the whim of some senior architect more interested in his own career than a cub designer. There'd be a lot of legwork, tons of grunt work, not only in designing and building models but in developing the actual building plans. And there would be all the legal filings and zoning and building codes he'd have to handle himself until he could afford to hire an assistant and find himself a couple of interns. Despite the uphill climb, he looked forward to the work, something he'd been missing the past few years.

And more importantly, there'd be no lies, no false promises, and no one lining their pockets on his talent and architectural vision.

He grabbed the mail from the box near the door and let himself into the house. After the success of the presentation, the quiet of the old Victorian felt anticlimactic. No one waited for him, anxious to hear about his presentation with the developer. No one greeted him with a saucy grin and promising sparkle in her green eyes.

He dropped his briefcase near the desk and frowned. Living alone had never been a problem. After living in Los Angeles for eight years, it had taken him a few weeks to reacquaint himself with sharing living space with his brother again. Now, the quiet unsettled him and had his thoughts traveling down a precarious path. Was he just missing having Austin around again, or was it Cait he wanted to find waiting for him when he came home?

The sound of the doorbell drew him back to the front of the house. He opened the door, hiding his disappointment when it wasn't Cait, but Travis Michaelson, one of Austin's employees.

"I was in the neighborhood," Travis said, opening the screen door. "I need that address for the bachelorette party Thursday night."

"It's in here." Jordan headed into the office, checked the schedule, then located the order form for the address. He still hadn't solved the double-booking problem since the guys he'd asked thus far had other plans following their fantasy obligations.

"Can you handle two fantasies in one night?" Jordan asked Travis, handing him a piece of scrap paper with the address on it. "Saturday night?"

Travis shrugged. "No problem. Med school isn't cheap, so I've doubled up before. What do they want?"

Jordan consulted the schedule, then picked up the phone when it rang. All week he'd taken order after order for various fantasies and couldn't help being amazed by the volume of business Fantasy for Hire generated. As proprietor, he knew his brother sometimes had to fill in during an emergency, which was how Austin and Teddy had met, but since Austin was now a married man, he understood his brother's need to sell the business. His sister-in-law, no matter how sweet, would no doubt have little appreciation for her husband fulfilling other women's fantasies.

He finished taking an order for a fantasy cowboy and hung up the phone. "You're an executive at seven," he said to Travis. "I need a vampire for a ten-o'clock engagement. Can you handle it?"

"Yeah, I can handle it," Travis agreed with a chuckle. "A vampire, huh? I've done some interesting fantasies, but never a vampire."

"I can't figure out women," Jordan muttered, giving Travis the addresses for both Saturday jobs.

Travis slipped the addresses into his wallet. "Hey, I've stopped trying. I decided to just enjoy the hell out of them, quirks and all."

Jordan crossed his arms over his chest. "You ever take the time to discover all the quirks about one woman?"

The young med student's smile faded. "I thought I would once, but it didn't work out."

"How'd you know?"

"That it wouldn't work out?"

Jordan shook his head. "That you wanted to find out more about her?"

"That's the easy part," Travis said, a rueful note in his voice. "I couldn't stop thinking about her."

That wasn't what Jordan wanted to hear. He'd been trying since he met Cait to shake her from his mind, but she was firmly planted within his consciousness.

Travis left and Jordan headed into the kitchen, looking for a cool drink, wondering how on earth Cait had managed to get under his skin. She remained an enigma, and every time he attempted to steer the conversation down a road of discovery, she promptly, and quite effectively, changed the subject. He was starting to think she was hiding something from him, but what or why, he was at a loss to understand.

With Cait Sullivan, he had more questions than he had answers, and he wasn't sure how he felt about that.

Popping open a cola, he spied the red light of the answering machine blinking rapidly and punched the Play button.

"Hey there, big brother."

A grin tugged Jordan's lips at the laughter in Austin's voice. His brother sounded happy, truly happy, and no matter how much that pleased him, he couldn't help feeling a slight twinge of envy. At least Austin's days of coming home to an empty house were over.

"Hi, Jordan!" Teddy's sweet voice joined Austin's. "I'm sorry we didn't catch you at home. Austin and I will be home Saturday around noon."

More laughter erupted from the recording, and Jordan shook his head in bemusement. Hopefully, the escrow on his condo in L.A. would close soon because his presence would definitely put a crimp in the newlyweds' life-style.

"If you're going to be around, we could use a lift from the airport," Austin said. "If you can't make it, don't sweat it. We'll take a cab. See ya later."

"Bye, Jor—" Teddy had started to say, before Austin severed the call.

The machine continued on to two hang-ups, a wrong number and three more hang-ups before he heard Cait's sultry voice.

"Hi, Jordan," she said. There was a brief pause followed by a rush of words he could barely decipher. He replayed the message and listened carefully.

"I - was - hoping - you'd - like - to - do - something - tonight. Dinner - and - a - movie. My - treat." Another long pause followed. "See you at seven?" It sounded more like a question than a request.

There it was, he thought with a frown. More contradictions. She'd obviously been nervous, and he couldn't help wondering if all those hang-ups on the answering machine had been Cait attempting to gather her courage to ask him on a date. It was almost as if he was dealing with two different women, and that made little sense. Who was the real Cait? The brazen siren who'd attempted to seduce him out of his mind, or the nervous, wholesome, penny-pinching girl next door who needed to gather her courage before asking him on a date?

He was determined to find out, one way or another. Because if he understood anything, it was that Cait Sullivan was in his life for more than just a valentine fantasy.

EITHER JORDAN was smarter than she'd given him credit for and could give lessons on cool and unruffled to the Secret Service, or he really didn't give a rip she supposedly could afford to buy her own small country.

She shook another Milk Dud from the super-large economy pack and tossed the candy into her mouth while casting a surreptitious glance in his direction. His attention was riveted on the final car-chase scene on the big screen, his arm slung lazily over the back of her seat as if the balance of her counterfeit checkbook made no difference to him whatsoever.

He *had* to take the bait, she thought in frustration. He just had to, or she had no story, not to mention had lost the opportunity to recoup the balance on her genuine bank statement, which was quite pitiful. Not once during dinner at the Chinese restaurant across the street from the multiplex theater had he so much as commented on the topic of spare change that collects under sofa cushions, let alone the balance of her simulated statements. He'd seen the file, since she'd purposely left it open on the table for his viewing pleasure, making certain the most mouthwatering of the lot was on top just in case he'd suffered from a sudden case of integrity. That bogus bank statement alone should have had him clamoring to bilk her of her fake fortune.

"Everything okay?" he whispered against her ear as the houselights rose.

She fought to suppress the delightful little shiver eddying down her spine and gave up the fight. She glanced up. "Fine, why?"

Using his thumb, he gently dragged it across her forehead. "You're frowning." He grinned, one of those sexy lopsided ones that always sent her pulse racing just a little faster.

"Just thinking of something I have to do tomorrow," she said. Like contact Louden Avery and tell him that as far as she could tell, the agency was legit, a look-but-don't-touch-the-merchandise kind of establishment.

Disappointment weighed heavily on her shoulders. She'd been positive that Jordan would have been salivating at the thought of getting his hands on her "money," but considering his absolute lack of reaction, she had no other choice but to tell Louden Avery first thing in the morning he was dead wrong about the McBride brothers.

"It's early yet," Jordan said, rising. "Let's go for a drive."

Cait stood and slipped on her jacket. The excitement and hope that he was offering to extend their evening so he could ask her for cold hard cash had waned, but she nodded in agreement anyway. She'd paid for this fantasy, she might as well enjoy it while it lasted—and get *her* money's worth.

Twenty minutes later, Jordan parked his truck to face the spectacular, and very romantic, moonlit view of San Francisco Bay. The night was surprisingly clear, and in the distance, Cait could easily make out the lights of the Presidio and the Golden Gate Bridge. She loved the city and couldn't imagine living anywhere else.

"Why did you leave San Francisco?" she asked, unbuckling her seat belt.

Jordan followed suit, then shifted in the black leather seat to face her. "I had a great offer from the firm in L.A.," he said. "Austin was all grown up and didn't need me around, so I took the job."

She rested her head against the back of the seat and looked into his hazel eyes reflecting the dimming glow of the illuminated dash lights. "What did your brother have to do with you leaving the city?"

He rested his arm on the back of the seat, the tips of his fingers absently brushing the curls near her ear. Maybe it was a good thing Jordan wasn't after her fake fortune, because she certainly did enjoy him touching her.

"Not long after I turned eighteen, my parents went away for a weekend to celebrate their twenty-fifth wedding anniversary. They were killed in a small-plane crash in the Sierra Nevadas. Austin's two years younger than me, so he became my responsibility, along with the house we both inherited."

Cait's heart went out to Jordan. She couldn't begin to imagine the pain of losing her parents, especially at such a young age. "I'm sorry. I didn't know."

He shrugged. "It was a long time ago," he said quietly.

Without thinking, she reached up and laced her fingers with his. "That must have been so hard on both of you. I mean, losing your parents is difficult enough, but having to raise your little brother couldn't have been easy on either one of you."

"We survived. Not that Austin made it a picnic," he said, a frown forming on his forehead.

She bit back a smile. "Bit of a rebel, was he?"

Jordan chuckled, the sound warm and intimate, setting off a series of shivers along her spine. "Something like that," he said, settling their joined hands in her lap. "Life would have been a lot easier if he'd been willing to listen to his older, and much wiser, brother."

"Don't be so hard on him," she said, struggling to keep her thoughts on the conversation, hoping for a glimpse into the lives of the McBride brothers. Maybe Jordan was everything he said, but his brother could be another matter altogether. Just her luck, she'd hired the wrong fantasy.

Jordan's hand was warm against the top of her jean-clad thigh, evaporating her investigative thoughts. All she could think about was their fingers laced intimately together, the press of his palm against hers and how perfectly her hand fit in his much larger one, making her curious about what other ways they would fit just as perfectly.

"I know how he feels," she said. "I'm the youngest and my sisters and oldest brother are always butting into my life."

He frowned, but there was no heat in his gaze, only affection for a brother he cared for deeply. "I wasn't butting in, but trying to make sure he stayed out of trouble—which wasn't always easy with Austin."

"But he turned out fine," she prompted, wondering if this might be the angle she needed to follow, since so far, Jordan had failed to cooperate. "I mean, he's not doing anything illegal, right?"

"Yeah. He turned out okay."

His gaze dipped to her mouth, and his eyes darkened slightly, kicking her pulse into overdrive. How was it that one look from Jordan could put her feminine senses on alert?

"Why are we talking about my little brother, when there are so many more interesting things we could be...discussing?" he asked, his voice dropping to a low, husky rumble that skittered along her nerve endings.

She shrugged. "I dunno," she whispered, because her voice had decided to take a leave of absence. Along with her senses, she silently added as she slowly leaned toward Jordan. Just one kiss, she told herself. "Why are we?"

"Beats me," he said. Using his other hand, he slipped it around the back of her neck and pulled her the remaining distance toward him.

"Jordan—"

"Shh. Let me kiss you, Cait."

She wouldn't dream of stopping him.

His mouth slipped over hers, and she opened to him, his tongue sliding across hers in erotic promise. Her heart thundered in her chest, and the warmth of pleasure cascaded through her. She cursed the console between them, the urge to press her body against his, to feel the contact of his body, suddenly overwhelming. He must have sensed her need, because he shifted, drawing them closer together.

She arched toward him and he dropped her hand, skimming his fingers along her hip, sliding upward beneath the hem of her sweater. His warm fingers brushed teasingly along her skin, easing up to cup her breast. She wreathed her arms around his neck, straining toward him, toward that contact she so desperately needed. A soft moan lodged in her throat, then finally escaped as his thumb rasped against the lace cup of her bra. A series of tingles shot through her and her nipples tightened, the conflicting sensations making her melt in his arms.

Sweet heaven, she'd never wanted a man the way she wanted Jordan. Her skin felt tight and hot, the desire to make love to him stronger than any emotion she'd ever known. The magic between them was more delicious, and a million times more satisfying, than any carton of comfort food on the market. The need to touch him, to make him feel the same fully charged sensations rippling through her in hot waves, to make him feel as mindless as she was feeling, drove her.

She slid her hand from around his neck, over his broad shoulder and down the firm wall of his chest. He pulled his mouth from hers, trailing hot kisses along her jaw until his tongue traced the delicate shell of her ear, making her tremble in his arms. Her breath came fast and hard, and she yearned to feel his skin, to explore his big body, not only with her hands, but with her own body. The thought of making love to Jordan frightened her as much as it excited her, but she knew she'd find a thrill ride of pure pleasure in his arms and in his bed.

Unable to resist the impulse to touch his skin, she worked the buttons on his shirt and slipped her hand inside the cotton fabric. The rough hair of his chest rasped against her palm, the warmth of his smooth, muscled skin drove her crazy, heightening her need for more.

His hand slid to her back and unfastened the hook of her bra. The heat of his hand cupping the weight of her breast was too much, and she shifted, rising to her knees in the bucket seat. A grinding, gnawing ache settled in her abdomen, filling her with a need so fierce she thought for certain she'd explode if she didn't make love to Jordan.

Ignoring Sister Cecilia's stern lectures to the eighth-grade girls at Saint Margaret's about car dates with boys, and the evils of premarital sex, Cait lifted her sweater, pushed her bra aside and stretched her body across the console to press her breasts against Jordan's chest.

A groan rose from inside him. One large hand

clamped her hip, while the other settled behind her head and guided her mouth back to his for another hot, openmouthed kiss that had her head spinning and her body clamoring for completion.

Until he broke the kiss.

She looked at him, confused. His eyes were dark and glazed with passion. The same thrum of desire had to be rippling through him. Didn't it? Wasn't he interested in the same sweet, sensual promise of satisfaction she was practically begging him to fulfill?

"I better take you home," he said, his voice a low, strained whisper.

"Why?" she asked, kissing his chin, then his chest, sliding her tongue along the opening of his shirt. He sucked in a sharp breath, and she smiled against the warmth of his belly.

"Because if I don't," he said, pulling her up to look into her eyes, "we're going to end up making love right here."

That got her attention. "And this is a problem?" she asked, reluctantly settling back into her own seat.

He reached toward her and cupped her cheek in his hand. "When we make love, Cait, and we will," he whispered in a voice filled with promise, "it's not going to be in the back seat like a couple of hormonal teenagers."

Cait adjusted her clothes as the warmth within her faded and reality settled around her. She didn't doubt Jordan's claim for a minute.

And realized with sudden clarity that she couldn't wait for the moment to arrive.

7

CAIT CHOSE a small table near the rear of Higher Grounds for her midmorning meeting with Louden Avery. He hadn't been happy when she'd called this meeting, but unless he had some concrete, verifiable evidence, or a very solid lead, she had no other choice but to shelve the story.

And find a way to tell Jordan the truth about the real Cait Sullivan.

The Cait Sullivan who was house-sitting for her brother, drove a car with enough accumulated mileage to have circled the globe twice, and was thrilled on those rare occasions when the balance due on her credit card was actually lower than her savings-account balance.

That Cait Sullivan carried her double-shot cappuccino to the table and sat facing the door to await Louden Avery's arrival. While she was disappointed the story hadn't worked out as she'd hoped, she told herself there'd be other stories, other great investigative opportunities to catapult her career.

She didn't think there'd be another Jordan McBride.

She blew on the steamed milk of her cappuccino and took a tentative sip. There was a connection between her and Jordan, a magical link, and that's what bore further investigation. She had no idea if Jordan was "the one," but she certainly wanted to take the time to find out. Unless she came clean with the truth now, she'd never know for certain. She expected him to be angry with her, possibly even hurt because she'd lied to him and used him, but he'd be even more so if she waited much longer to confess.

Jen was right, she thought, dipping the edge of her biscotti into the steamed, foamy milk. She could very well lose her own piece of the fairy tale. And for what? A story that had gone as sour as Geraldo's venture into Al Capone's vault?

When Jordan had dropped her off last night, after another mind-blowing kiss at the door that had her wanting him all over again, he'd told her to be ready for romance tonight. Somewhere along the way, the fantasy had taken a back seat to reality, the reality that there was more to her relationship with Jordan than her hiring him to be her valentine fantasy or looking for a story that didn't exist. And tonight, she'd bring reality crashing down around them because she had no choice but to tell him the truth before they went any further. If there was a chance they could have a serious relationship, and she was about as certain as a girl could get at this point, then it was time to fess up, and hope like the devil he could forgive her for being a low-down, dirty liar.

She groaned inwardly. How could he ever forgive her? She'd lied to him.

You're a slug, Sullivan.

She *was* a slug, she thought in agreement, taking a bite of biscotti.

You're so low you have to look up to see an ant's belly.

He'd hate her forever. She'd used him to advance her career. She was no better than the partners of the firm that had used him.

You're like that crusty white stuff that accumulates on the corner of your mouth when you're really thirsty.

"All right, that's enough," she muttered, dipping her cookie into the cappuccino again.

He'll never forgive you.

She sighed and took another small bite of biscotti. He might, if she presented her defense well.

She took another bite of the gourmet cookie and looked up as Louden walked through the double glass doors. The fading bruises that had given him the appearance of a jaundiced racoon had disappeared, and he was dressed just as neatly as he'd been the day he'd first come to her with the lead. He didn't bother to stop at the counter to place an order, but came directly to her table and pulled out a chair.

"What's so important, Ms. Sullivan, that you couldn't tell me over the phone?" he asked, his voice filled with impatience.

She set the cookie on the edge of the saucer and folded her hands in front of her on the Formica table. "There's no story, Mr. Avery. I don't know where you obtained your facts, but based on the information I've been able to gather, there is nothing underhanded, illegal, or even remotely inappropriate about the services offered by Fantasy for Hire. I'm sorry."

His blue eyes narrowed and he leaned forward. There was something about him that made her glad she'd arranged this meeting in a public place. It wasn't anything she could actually pinpoint, just a menacing quality slight enough to put her on guard.

PLAY "LUCKY 7" AND GET
THREE FREE GIFTS!

HOW TO PLAY:

1. With a coin, carefully scratch off the silver box at the right. Then check the claim cha see what we have for you — **FREE BOOKS** and a gift — **ALL YOURS! ALL FREE!**

2. Send back this card and you'll receive brand-new Harlequin Temptation® novels. Th books have a cover price of $3.99 each in the U.S. and $4.50 each in Canada, but they yours to keep absolutely free.

3. There's no catch. You're ur no obligation to buy anything. charge nothing — ZERO — your first shipment. And you d have to make any minimum num of purchases — not even one!

4. The fact is thousands of readers enjoy receiving books by mail from the Harlequin Rea Service®. They enjoy the convenience of home delivery... they like getting the best novels at discount prices, BEFORE they're available in stores... and they love their *Hea Heart* newsletter featuring author news, horoscopes, recipes, book reviews and much more

5. We hope that after receiving your free books you'll want to remain a subscriber. the choice is yours — to continue or cancel, any time at all! So why not take us up on invitation, with no risk of any kind. You'll be glad you did!

YOURS FREE!

PLAY LUCKY 7 FOR THIS EXCITING FREE GIFT!

THIS SURPRISE MYSTERY GIFT COULD BE YOURS FREE WHEN YOU PLAY

LUCKY 7!

Visit us on-line at
www.romance.net

NO COST! NO OBLIGATION TO BUY!
NO PURCHASE NECESSARY!

The Harlequin Reader Service® — Here's how it works:

Accepting your 2 free books and gift places you under no obligation to buy anything. You may keep the books and gift and return the shipping statement marked "cancel." If you do not cancel, about a month later we'll send you 4 additional novels and bill you just $3.34 each in the U.S., or $3.80 each in Canada, plus 25¢ delivery per book and applicable taxes if any.* That's the complete price and — compared to cover prices of $3.99 each in the U.S. and $4.50 each in Canada — it's quite a bargain! You may cancel at any time, but if you choose to continue, every month we'll send you 4 more books, which you may either purchase at the discount price or return to us and cancel your subscription.

*Terms and prices subject to change without notice. Sales tax applicable in N.Y. Canadian residents will be charged applicable provincial taxes and GST.

"Then I suggest you dig deeper," he said in an icy tone. "I know for a fact that one of my former employees exchanged cash for sex. Obviously you're not looking in the right place."

He'd told her this before, but as far as she could tell, there was nothing inappropriate about Austin McBride's fantasy venture. Considering all the bait she'd used, if Jordan had been a trout, he'd have been hooked, landed, rolled in cracker meal and panfried in butter by now. He just wasn't biting.

Reaching into her purse, she pulled out a notepad, doubting Louden had new information, but unwilling to let go until she was certain.

"How did you learn about the exchange?"

He straightened and looked down his slightly crooked nose at her. "I've already told you about the receipt for services rendered," he snapped.

She jotted a few notes on the pad. "Do you have a copy of this receipt?"

He shook his head. "Unfortunately, no. But if you can find it, you'll have all the verification you need."

"How do you propose I do that?" she asked with a frown. "It's not like I have access to the financial records of the agency."

"Then I suggest you find a way," he suggested in the same icy tone he'd used earlier.

She set her pen on the pad and looked at him as if he'd lost his mind. "Are you suggesting I do something illegal?"

He shrugged his shoulders. "Whatever it takes. Isn't that the reporter's creed?"

Cait bit the inside of her lip. Could she let it go? If she didn't, she'd never know if the magic between her and Jordan was real. If she continued, whether or not she found the verification necessary to go to print, she'd lose Jordan forever.

She rested her elbows on the table and pressed the tips of her fingers together. Maybe, just maybe, after their romantic evening, she could suggest they go back to his place. His brother operated Fantasy for Hire out of the house. *If* the opportunity presented itself, she'd see if she could find some shred of evidence that would support Louden's allegation. If she turned up nothing, as she suspected, and hoped, then she'd be spending the rest of the evening confessing the truth to Jordan. Confessing and praying he'd find it in his heart to forgive her.

She needed more to go on and knew it. "It's not enough," she told Louden finally. "That receipt you claim exists could be for anything."

His pale eyes narrowed and he leaned forward. "What if I told you I overheard a conversation that explicitly spelled out the terms of the services rendered?"

Cait bit her lip. "Did you?"

Louden leaned back in the chair and looked smug. "Perhaps."

Now it was Cait's turn to narrow her eyes. "Perhaps isn't good enough, Mr. Avery."

"Austin McBride is out of town this week. How else would I know that unless I overheard his conversation with my employee, who also happens to be on vacation. You can check it out yourself. All you have to do is call the ad agency and see that I'm telling you the truth."

Her heart sank. Austin *was* out of town. Jordan had

told her so himself. Avery knew too much for it to be a coincidence, but still, without that receipt...

Disheartened, she stuffed her notepad back into her purse and stood. "I'll give it one more try. If I find nothing concrete, then I'm afraid there will be no story. I can't go to press without verification."

She slung her bag over her shoulder and looked down at Louden Avery. "That, Mr. Avery, is *this* reporter's creed."

SINCE SHE'D BEEN CAST in the role of wealthy seductress for one last performance, Cait decided to liberate Brian's Lexus as a prop for her grand finale. As she parked the luxury car on the street in front of the Victorian house Jordan and Austin had inherited from their parents, she didn't regret her decision to drive it.

The neighborhood was old and established, and she noted that many of the turn-of-the-century Victorian homes lining the immaculate street could be described as no less than stately. Not exactly fitting surroundings for her fifteen-year-old hatchback.

She wasn't certain what Jordan had planned for tonight other than what he'd alluded to in his message on her answering machine—roses and romance...at *his* place. At least her problem of trying to convince him to take her back to his house had been solved, she thought as she cut the engine.

She looked up at the house, wondering how on earth she was going to find the proof she needed, or worse, tell Jordan the truth. The warm, welcoming glow of the porch light illuminated the concrete walkway that led to a set of wooden steps, but she felt anything but warm. She felt cold inside because, either way, any relationship with Jordan would likely end tonight.

She left the car and headed toward the steps, where she found deep red and creamy-white rose petals littering the steps. Despite the dread that had been churning in her stomach all afternoon in anticipation of tonight, she followed the trail up the steps to the front door. The door had been left ajar, so she pushed it open and entered the foyer.

She noticed two things. The heavenly scent of fresh sourdough bread, and the office where she'd first propositioned Jordan. Inside the darkened room, she spied a couple of old file cabinets she was pretty certain would hold the financial records of the agency. If a receipt existed, or maybe a schedule or journal to confirm Avery's latest allegation, that's where she'd find them. Only the path of petals led into what must have at one time been an old-fashioned parlor used for greeting guests, to a flight of stairs leading to the upper level.

She slowly climbed the carpeted staircase. Trailing her hand along the mahogany banister, she followed the petal path, smiling to herself at how he'd methodically alternated single red and white petals on each step up to the landing above. She didn't know another man who would have gone to such lengths to warm her heart.

No one except Jordan.

Ignoring the stab of guilt, she followed the petals scattered along the landing to the front part of the upper level, stopping at an open doorway.

She peered inside and her breath caught.

In all her life, she'd never seen a more romantic setting, nor did she think she'd ever have the pleasure of viewing one again.

The scent of roses drew her farther into the octagon-shaped room. An unaccustomed rush of tears briefly burned the backs of her eyes. She blinked, only to open them to stare in disbelief at the dozens of long-stemmed, red and white roses lying on the chintz cushion of the window seat. On an antique bureau sat two large, lead-crystal vases of roses in front of an etched triptych precisely angled to create an illusion of hundreds more of the beautiful, scented buds.

She stepped carefully over the petals scattered on the carpeting to the center of the room. Pristine white linen topped a small, round table set with platinum-rimmed china and elegantly carved crystal goblets. The flickering light from two long, red tapers added to the soft, romantic glow, the only other light seeping into the room from the yellowed fog lamps in the street below.

Her heart ached as she moved closer to the table. A bottle of white wine, no doubt expertly chosen as the perfect accompaniment, sat in a bucket of ice. Warm crusty sourdough rolls nestled inside a wicker basket, which were wrapped with care in a linen napkin. She had no doubt he'd planned every detail of the meal to tantalize even the most discriminating palate. But all this paled in comparison to the significance of the single red rose laid across one of the place settings.

"It's just an illusion," she whispered, tracing the tip of her finger along the delicate, velvet bud. All part of the fantasy she'd paid Jordan to create. She refused to believe it meant anything else.

A whisper of sound caught her attention. She looked up, her gaze catching Jordan's in the reflection of the center panel of the etched mirror. "Everything is so beautiful," she said quietly.

He came up behind her, gently settling his hands on her shoulders. "You're beautiful," he said, his eyes filled with an intensity that sent her pulse careening and her heart pounding in a heavy rhythm.

It's just a fantasy. It's just a fantasy.

His warm breath brushed her ear, followed by the seductive press of his lips against the nape of her neck, sending a dose of reality skittering down her spine.

She stiffened and moved away from his distracting touch, crossing the room to the window overlooking the lights of the bay in the distance. Wrapping her arms around her middle, she briefly closed her eyes. She needed strength if she was going to survive the evening, because, right now, she wanted nothing more than to lose herself in the fantasy. Wine, candlelight, the heady perfume of roses, Vivaldi's *Spring* playing softly on the CD player and a man who set her soul on fire with a simple brush of his lips against her skin were proving a difficult, and all too tempting, distraction from her goal.

"I hope you brought your appetite."

She opened her eyes and glanced at him over her shoulder. Oh, she had an appetite all right, but not the kind appeased by anything edible. "Seafood?" she asked with more sass than she was feeling.

He chuckled, the sound warm and inviting. "Only

the best," he countered, reaching for the wine. He poured them each a glass, then handed her one of the crystal glasses.

"To the fantasy?" she asked, lifting her glass.

He shook his head. "To us," he said, then waited for her to touch her glass to his.

The response clogged in her throat. He didn't mean it. Just because he was saying and doing all the right things to make a girl seriously consider throwing herself in his arms and begging him to carry her off into the proverbial sunset, didn't mean it meant anything. "To us" was as make-believe as the hungry look in his darkening eyes and nothing more than another clause in their agreement. She'd paid him to create a romantic fantasy, and he was fulfilling his contractual obligation—in spades!

She gave him what she hoped was a seductive grin, then lifted her glass to his before taking a sip. Only sheer determination kept her from downing the Chardonnay like a shot of Cuervo with a lime chaser.

"You certainly went to a lot of trouble," she said, her gaze sweeping the room.

Jordan breathed in the alluring aroma of Cait's perfume, wanting nothing more than to discover for himself which of her little pulse points she'd dabbed with the beguiling scent.

He shrugged. "I enjoyed preparing it," he said, setting his glass on the table. Slowly, he closed the distance between them. She looked up at him, her big, green eyes filled with questions, apprehension, and something else he couldn't quite determine.

He shrugged it off and slipped the wineglass from

her trembling fingers. "Are you nervous?" he asked, unable to keep the amusement out of his voice.

She arched her eyebrows and gave him a saucy grin. "What makes you say that?" She might have been able to pull off the spunk if her voice hadn't shook and her eyes hadn't darted around the room.

He slipped his hands over the black silky material of her dress, settling them on her gently rounded hips, and pulled her toward him until he could feel the heat of her body. Her hands landed on his chest, and her eyes rounded in surprise. "Because I'm going to kiss you. You always look nervous just before I kiss you."

Her tongue darted out to moisten her bottom lip. "Don't be ridiculous."

The innocent move sent a flash of heat through his body. "There's nothing ridiculous about the way you make me feel, Cait."

"Jordan, there's some—"

"Shh," he whispered, then captured her lips in an openmouthed kiss hot enough to scorch them both.

His tongue gathered her hot, sweet flavor, while his hands rocked her closer. She moaned softly, then curled her fingers into the cotton of his shirt. If she thought he was going anywhere, she was gravely mistaken.

He was playing with fire, but dousing the flames licking through him was next to impossible. She'd been driving him crazy since she'd walked into his life four days ago, and while he had every intention of adhering to the agreement they'd made, he was inches away from tossing aside his noble intentions and giving in to the powerful longing that had been plaguing him since he'd met her.

She might be out for fun and games, but that didn't stop him from wanting her. When he'd picked her up for the movie the previous evening, he'd had to wait for her to finish dressing. He knew she didn't work for a living, she'd said as much on their first "date"— but he'd been unprepared for the magnitude of her life of luxury when he'd caught an unintentional glimpse of her financial statements.

He knew Cait wanted him. He didn't doubt for a minute there wasn't some sort of connection between them, but what he couldn't get past was that she wasn't only rich, but extremely wealthy. And he was basically unemployed.

Those thoughts left his mind in favor of more pleasurable thoughts when she looped her arms around his neck, pressing her delectable body against his. He forgot about balance sheets and invoices. All that mattered was her mouth, and all the soft and warm and moist secrets he collected on his tongue.

He had two choices. Stop the sweet torture now or surrender to the desire pounding through him. As much as he wanted the latter, he ended the kiss and gently set her away from him. He didn't want to play games with her. He wanted her, heart, body and soul. If she'd have him, employment status and all.

The tenderness in her eyes tugged at his heart, convincing him they did stand a chance, despite the obstacles. Her slightly swollen lips and the gentle rise and fall of her breasts pressing against the black silk of her dress fanned an already blazing inferno within him.

"Dinner," he said firmly, then turned to pull out a chair for her before he followed through on the more base instincts clamoring inside him. He was determined to talk to her tonight. A serious discussion that included a relationship beyond being her hired valentine. All day he'd been unable to concentrate on the sketches he'd been attempting to draw or on the constant phone calls for the agency. His thoughts had continually returned to the figures he'd seen in that open file and the fear creeping into him that it could make a difference in their future—if they even had a future together.

The sexy grin canting her lips distracted him as she moved to the chair and sat. Carefully, and he was damned sure deliberately, she crossed her legs, causing the silky material to inch up, exposing her slim thighs. "I can't wait to see what's next on the menu," she said, her voice filled with sin. She slicked her tongue over her bottom lip. "The appetizer was quite...tasty."

He leaned forward, his mouth hovering inches from hers until he could smell her sweet breath and the tangy essence of wine on her lips. "That was nothing compared to the main course."

The promise of pleasure burning in her eyes could only be resisted by a will of iron. Too bad his suddenly felt about as flexible as a cheap aluminum can.

8

THE LOBSTER BISQUE was delicious, as was the shrimp scampi, but not half as scrumptious as the lingering sweetness of Cait's lips or the soft, gentle glow of all that exposed skin glistening in the candlelight. Jordan wanted to taste that sweet mouth again, he ached to smooth his hands over her body, not only tonight, or tomorrow, but for many more tomorrows.

Good God, he was starting to sound like a lovesick fool. If Austin had an inkling that his brother was mooning over a woman, Jordan would never hear the end of it. Considering the bad time he'd given Austin for falling for Teddy, he was certain his little brother would find the retribution far too enjoyable.

He still didn't know how it had happened, but there was no denying he was falling hard for Cait, contradictions and all. While he wasn't exactly ready to pick out china, neither could he deny that the possibilities with her were endless. Unanswered questions aside, he wanted her in his life. To what extent, he couldn't be sure...yet. What he was feeling went beyond her sweet smile and the way her nose crinkled up all cute and sexy when she laughed. The way she closed her eyes and moaned when she bit into a rich, buttery piece of seafood inspired his imagination. The way she pressed against him when they kissed jump-started his libido. The way she looked at him, as if she wanted to eat him alive, drove him crazy with need.

The way she kept casting surreptitious glances at him over the candlelight made him nervous as hell.

She flirted, as she always did, but her smile wasn't as quick and easy, and the teasing light he'd become so accustomed to in her eyes had been replaced with worry.

Something was on her mind.

He pushed the scampi through the garlic-and-herb butter on his plate and looked at her. She'd been too quiet through the appetizer. She hadn't uttered a word when he'd served the lobster bisque. Other than the appreciative glint in her eyes when he'd set a serving of scampi and rice pilaf with fresh buttered scallops in front of her, she'd been distant throughout the meal. Even now her eyes were downcast as she stared unseeingly at the floral centerpiece, her wispy auburn bangs barely covering the frown creasing her forehead.

He set his fork on the plate. "What's on your mind, Cait?"

Her fingers, absently stroking the stem of the wine-glass, stilled. She looked up. Regret clouded her gaze.

She let out a long breath and flashed him a grin he suspected was anything but honest. "Is this part of the fantasy?" she asked abruptly.

He frowned. "What do you mean?" Caution gripped him. He might have started out creating a fantasy for her, but he had to admit that he was having serious thoughts of exchanging fantasy for reality. He wanted her, and his willpower to wait until he'd fulfilled their contract before he pursued a serious relationship with her was slowly crumbling. She'd gotten under his skin, even if he knew next to nothing about her.

Her grin faded. "How real is this?" she asked quietly. "Is this just another contractual obligation under the wish-fulfillment clause, or is there something more going on here that I should know about?"

Oh, there was a lot more going on, of that he had no doubt. Just how much, he'd yet to determine. "Does it matter?"

She set her fork aside and folded her hands primly in front of her on the linen tablecloth. "That's my problem. I don't know if this is supposed to matter or not, but I think it does."

Her confession surprised him. He'd been wrestling with the issue for the better part of the week. Was she only in this for fun and games, a poor little rich girl out for a little walk on the wild side? Or was she feeling the same heart-stopping emotion? "Do you want it to mean something more?" he asked carefully.

She looked at him over the soft glow of the burning candles. Her gaze held caution...and hope. "I think I do, but there's something..."

He sighed when she left the words dangling between them. He knew where this was leading, and he couldn't blame her. If he was in her position, he'd have more than a few concerns, but he hoped it wouldn't be an issue between them.

"But something has you feeling a little cautious," he finished for her. Well, he was feeling a bit cautious himself, because he needed to know who the hell Cait

Sullivan was. He was falling for her, hard, and he didn't know anything about her.

"Something like that," she admitted and looked away.

No time like the present, he thought, pushing his plate aside. "Is it the money?" They needed to discuss the fact that she was filthy rich and he was struggling. Even if he wasn't exactly destitute, his financial status was a joke in comparison.

Her gaze snapped to his, suddenly clear and bright. "Money?" she asked with a lift of her delicately arched eyebrow.

He almost wished he'd never seen the file with her financial statements. But he had, and he thought it best if they waded through the issue of her fortune now before they both became completely lost in the fantasy.

"I apologize, Cait. When you were changing last night, I happened to see the folder you left open on the table downstairs. Look, I know I'm not exactly on the same financial footing as you, but you've got to believe me when I tell you that your money isn't an issue for me."

She cocked her head slightly to the side, her curls brushing against her cheek. "It's not?"

He shrugged. "Why should it be?"

"You're saying it doesn't make any difference to you. If I've got zillions of dollars or if I live paycheck to paycheck, it doesn't matter. You—"

"I want you, sweetheart, not your bank balance." He reached across the table and settled his hand over her folded ones. "Cait," he said, running his thumb over her smooth-as-silk skin, "I know what it's like to be used, remember? I know how it feels to be taken advantage of, and that's something you'd never have to worry about from me."

Something flashed in her gaze that made him wary. Guilt?

He shrugged it off, convinced his imagination had taken a wrong turn. Cait had nothing to feel guilty about.

"I don't have a crystal ball," he continued. "I can't tell you what's in the future for us, but you need to know it doesn't matter to me what your background is—rich, working class or dirt poor. You're what matters to me."

"I am?"

"Yeah, you are."

For the first time that night, she graced him with a radiant smile. Then she picked up her fork and did some serious damage to the meal he'd painstakingly prepared just for her.

TWENTY MINUTES and her second glass of Chardonnay later, Cait still hadn't found the right words to tell Jordan she wasn't one of San Francisco's who's who, but instead, a working woman with goals and dreams of her own...who'd been using him to further her career. She knew the longer she waited the more difficult it was going to be, which did nothing to persuade her conscience to spout the truth. The only truth she was interested in at the moment had to do with Jordan's admission, something she reluctantly acknowledged she knew all along. Jordan might be the perfect ingredient to fire up a girl's fantasy, but he was as "real" as it got.

"What's your schedule like tomorrow morning?" Jordan asked suddenly.

She reached for her wine. "I'm covering the opening of a new animal shelter," she blurted, then realized her mistake too late.

Confusion etched his expression. "Covering?"

She set the glass back on the table. "Well, you know what I mean," she said with a nervous wave, hoping he didn't see how badly her hand shook. "I'll...be there...is all I meant. Did I tell you these scallops are heavenly?" She wouldn't, couldn't look at him as she spoke, else he'd see guilt written all over her face in bright neon letters. Instead she concentrated on digging more scallops from the rice.

"Thanks," he said. "I think I saw something in the paper about it," he said. "Isn't the shelter being sponsored by some dog club?"

"The San Francisco Kennel Club." The tempo of her pulse picked up speed that, for once, had nothing to do with her forbidden attraction to Jordan, and everything to do with the six-foot grave she was digging for herself.

"I didn't know you had show dogs."

"I don't, I..."

Think, Sullivan. Think fast.

"I just like the shows is all, so I...support the effort."

"Can't say I've ever been to one."

"You're not missing much," she muttered and glanced up at him, curiosity brimming his gaze.

"Then why go?" he asked, topping off her wineglass.

Her mind spun. Yes, why indeed?

"I haven't really thought about it," she managed to say around the tightness of her throat. She wondered briefly what he'd think if she grabbed the wine bottle from him and chugged it dry. Probably no worse than he already did if he'd been paying serious attention to her lame responses.

"Anyway, you had something more exciting in mind?" she prompted, praying he'd take the bait and change the subject before she compounded the situation with more lies.

Thankfully, he chuckled. "I wouldn't exactly call it exciting, but I've made an appointment with a Realtor in town tomorrow morning to look at a few condos. I was wondering if you'd be interested in going with me."

"You're moving?" She set her fork on the plate and looked at him. "I thought you and your brother lived here."

He moved his plate aside and braced his arms on the table. "The house belongs to both of us, but Austin and his new bride are coming home from their honeymoon in a couple of days. The escrow on my condo in L.A. is closing soon, so the time is right. As it is, I'll probably be cramping the newlyweds' style for another couple of months until the escrow closes on whatever I find locally."

Alarm tripped through her. Married? Something was wrong. Horribly wrong. How could Fantasy for Hire be a front for a fortune-bilking scam if its proprietor was happily wed?

"Honeymoon?" she said, despite the sudden pounding in her chest. "As in, your brother's a married man?"

Jordan nodded and reached for his wine. "You sound surprised," he said before taking a drink.

Damned right she was surprised, and angry for believing Louden Avery and nearly ruining her chance at happiness. No wonder Austin was out of town for a week. The man was on his honeymoon!

"I just thought, you know, with a business like Fantasy for Hire, that...well, it just doesn't seem like the kind of thing a married man would do for a living."

"Austin always had been the quintessential bachelor, until recently. He started Fantasy for Hire after college, but it's always only been a sideline for him. He's been trying to sell it ever since his landscaping business started to boom."

"Selling the business," she muttered. Louden Avery had wanted her to find proof... Well, as far as she was concerned, she had more than enough...to shelve the story for good.

Surprisingly, the thought of losing her grand exposé didn't fill her with as much disappointment as she'd believed it would. Instead of mourning the loss of a career boost, she felt downright giddy at the possibilities. If Jordan was telling her the absolute truth, then not only was Fantasy for Hire legitimate, it made sense that *he* was everything *he* claimed—just a guy struggling to start his own business after being burned by the greedy, lying partners of his former firm.

"The agency's served its purpose," he said, pushing back his chair. "Austin started the business when he and a few of his buddies needed extra cash to pay off their college debts. I don't think he ever expected it to take off the way it did."

He stood and slowly moved toward the CD player. He flipped a switch and the classical music they'd been enjoying for most of the evening changed to the deep sultry voice of Aaron Neville singing an old blues tune.

As much as she tried, she couldn't keep the silly grin from her lips even if her heartbeat was pounding like thunder. If anyone had told her she'd be grinning like a fool because she'd been wrong about something that had been so important to her, she'd have laughed in their face.

But then her smile faded. She still had to tell him the truth. Now, before things became even more complicated between them.

He crossed the room and reached for her hand. "Let's not talk about my brother," he said, his voice taking on that deep, velvety quality that never failed to send a dance of delight skittering down her spine.

He laced their fingers together. She sucked in a deep breath and looked up to see a sexy glint canting his eyes. "That's good," she said, "because there's something I should tell you about before—"

He tugged on her hand and pulled her to her feet. "I'm not interested in talking, Cait."

Her heart faltered, then resumed at a maddening pace. "Oh," was all she could manage once his eyes darkened, signaling he was about to kiss her senseless. She knew exactly what he wanted to do. And blast her lying soul, what she planned on raising wasn't an objection.

He pulled her close, his arm banding her waist, his large, warm hand settling on the small of her back. "Dance with me?" he asked, but already he was gliding her away from the table and the remains of their meal to sway enticingly to the mournful blues tune.

Her breath caught at the emotion banked in his gaze as he looked at her. Delicious magic wove around them, and for the moment, Cait could think of nothing more urgent to tell Jordan than that she wanted him. She'd never been shy in her life, since being outspoken was a means of survival as the youngest of five siblings.

"I want you, Jordan," she whispered. She'd tell him the truth later, when she wasn't close enough to feel the heat of his body, or close enough to draw in the warm, male scent of him.

He moved their joined hands to his shoulder and slipped her fingers from his, then shifted their bodies even closer. The promise of pleasure lighting his eyes, and the feel of his body against hers left no mistake that he wanted her, and had her temperature climbing several degrees.

He didn't say anything, just slipped his hand behind her head and guided her lips to his. The first brush of his mouth on hers sent a thrum of desire rippling along her nerve endings. The second, deeper kiss made her senses spin with a rush of excitement. When he finally slanted his mouth over hers and cajoled her tongue to mate with his, any thought of suppressing the desire igniting between them died a quiet death.

She tasted like a fresh, summer rain, and Jordan felt like a man dying of thirst who couldn't get enough of her heavenly offering. She wanted him, but something had shifted, and he knew that later he'd be able to analyze exactly what had happened tonight. But right now all he could think about was the achingly feminine body pressing against him in silent invitation.

He tore his lips from hers and moved them along her satiny cheek to outline the delicate edge of her ear. She made a little purr of sound that heated his blood and had the grinding, gnawing ache in his stomach shifting south. If he didn't stop them soon, even his lousy moral code would be hard-pressed to ignore the demands of his body, and hers.

"I have to touch you," she whispered in hot demand, her lips pressing against his throat.

Instead of finding the words to stop her as her deft fingers worked the buttons of his shirt, he dipped his head to nuzzle her neck. As she slid her cool palms over his torso, the sweet agony of her gentle touch had him forgetting about contractual obligations and moving them toward the window seat, where he gently eased them down upon the chintz cushion.

"You're making me crazy," he admitted, taking little biting nips at her throat, then soothing them with his tongue.

Her responding chuckle was filled with enough sin to make a Benedictine monk question his vow of chastity. He didn't know what it was about Cait that did it to him, but each encounter with her left him craving her warm, willing body with a deeper intensity than the last time. Every time he got near her, his control slipped further and further. But tonight was different. Tonight, the throbbing of his lower body screamed in protest to his stupid moral code. Tonight, driving desire plunged him closer to the danger zone, and he honestly didn't know if the tenuous grip he'd managed to keep on his control thus far would be enough to stop them from making love.

"Touch me, Jordan." Her hot breath fanned his neck. "Please."

He groaned, powerless against her sweet demand. Capturing her mouth in a hot, openmouthed kiss, he slid his hands over her slim waist and down her gently rounded hips to the hem of her silky dress. He reached beneath the hem to caress her thigh, his fingers brushing against the tops of her stockings. His control took a dive when he slid his hand over the strap of a garter, his fingers brushing the outline of a satin bow. If it was red, like ripe summer strawberries, he was definitely a goner.

The soft, warm flesh of her thighs nearly had him coming out of his skin. But that was nothing compared to what he felt when he found the moist heat hidden behind the lace of her panties and when she arched toward his hand in a silent plea for more.

With a low, throaty growl, he slipped his arm behind her and moved them so she was straddling his lap. Her heavy-lidded eyes glowed emerald with passion. He was already rock-hard, but the sight of her slightly parted and swollen lips had him pulsing achingly with need. He slid his hands around her back to the zipper of her dress. Slowly, he pulled it down, the sound rasping along his nerves and louder than the old love song on the stereo.

He sucked in a sharp breath when he pushed the sleeves of her dress down, the black silk slithering past her shoulders and pooling at her waist, exposing her full, unencumbered breasts. "You're so beautiful," he managed to say around the dryness in his throat.

She smiled, one of those sultry, sexy ones that never failed to make his heart pound just a little harder. Her nipples tightened, and she reached for his hand and guided it to her breast. He didn't need any further encouragement, and when he palmed the feminine globe in his hand, she issued a soft little moan that had him mentally counting to ten in a vain attempt to regain control.

He dragged his thumb across her nipple, and she closed her eyes and rocked her hips forward. Her hands gripped his shoulders while her thighs gripped his hips as her body sought more intimate contact. He drew one dusky-rose nipple into his mouth and felt her fingers press into his shoulders. Her hips rocked forward again, this time more insistent. With one hand pressed against her very feminine posterior, he slipped the other beneath the pool of black satin to the scrap of lace, slipping his fingers beneath the elastic band to her hot, slick feminine folds. She cried out and tossed her auburn cap of curls back, her body arching. When he slid his fingers inside her, he was lost.

"You're so wet."

"Jordan," she cried, her voice a mix of strangled cry and whispered need. "I need you."

"Shh, sweetheart. I'll take you there."

She arched against his hand, and a soft, honeyed growl escaped her parted lips. Using his thumb, he drew the tension tighter while his fingers continued to draw more of her moist heat until she was trembling against him. He knew the moment her orgasm peaked as her body clenched tightly around him and her hands dived into his hair to pull his lips to hers. She became the aggressor, taking his mouth hard and hot and wet, using her tongue in ways that had his imagination working overtime. The soft, little mewling sounds she made as she slowly came back down to earth threatened to drive him over the edge, yet he didn't have the heart, or the will, to stop her sensual assault.

When she finally ended the kiss, she curled against him. He smoothed his hands down her back, holding her close, placing soft, teasing kisses against her temple.

"I can't believe you did that," she said, her voice sounding as if she'd just rolled out of bed.

His bed, he thought possessively, and knew that was exactly where he wanted her, and not on a temporary basis either. He wanted to wake up beside her in the mornings, wanted to come home to her at night. He wanted to share the day-to-day living, the everyday, the mundane, the kind of things that Austin would have with Teddy, the kind of life his parents had shared.

He was nuts.

He wasn't thinking straight.

How could he want those kind of things when he hardly knew her?

But he did.

He wanted them, and her, bad.

"I could say the same to you," he teased, and she laughed. He shifted so he could look into her eyes, masculine pride rearing up inside him at the com-

pletely satisfied, sleepy expression in her gaze as she
snuggled closer.

"That was...incredible," she said, planting a quick
kiss on his lips.

He chuckled. "Sweetheart, trust me. That was only
the beginning."

Curiosity got the better of him, and he slid his hand
to her thigh and pushed back the silk of her dress still
bunched around her waist. He bent to take a look at
the bows on her garter.

He dropped his head back against the mahogany
window frame, closed his eyes and groaned.

They were red...like ripe summer strawberries.

9

CAIT COULDN'T MOVE. Her body was filled with lethargic bliss caused by the incredible sensations Jordan had so effortlessly created. Since she had no intention of going anywhere at the moment, she curled her body closer to the comfort he offered and smoothed her hand over the sculpted wall of his chest, reveling in the feel of the hard, warm, male flesh beneath her palm. She still couldn't believe what they'd done, but she'd never been particularly shy and she wasn't about to start now.

Shy, never. Honest, well, that's another story.

She closed her eyes, but the action did nothing to quell her conscience. Telling herself she didn't want to disturb the peaceful afterglow didn't quiet the little voice inside her either. She knew what she had to do, and as much as she dreaded telling him the truth, she hated the thought of losing this wonderful moment even more.

Later. She'd definitely tell him later.

Jordan's hand drew lazy patterns over her hip and along her thigh, adding to the feeling of contentment, and heightening her guilt. As much as she attempted to convince her conscience otherwise, she couldn't help the feeling that what had just transpired between them was a lie, as deceitful as the role she'd been playing since she'd met him.

But it couldn't be a lie, she silently argued. How could her growing feelings for Jordan be anything but the truth? How could something so completely honest and beautiful be labeled deceitful? Hadn't he said that tonight was real?

And she was going to destroy whatever magic had occurred between them, irrevocably. The longer she waited, the bigger chance she had of losing him...forever.

"About tomorrow," she started, gently sifting her fingers through the sable curls covering his chest.

His arm tightened around her and the hand that had been absently massaging her hip and thigh crept upward to tip her face toward his. "Forget tomorrow," he murmured before placing quick little kisses at the corner of her mouth. "Let's concentrate on now."

He kissed her, long and deep, hard and wet. She moved his shirt aside and arched against him, rubbing her breasts against the smooth, hard width of his chest. Instantly, the subsiding heat resurfaced. Revelations and confessions took a back seat to the bone-melting mindlessness sweeping through her at a rapid rate.

Until the insistent ringing of the doorbell intruded.

He stiffened and pulled back. Straightening, he pushed back the corner of the lace curtain to peer out to the street. After a muffled curse, he kissed her one last time, then set her gently off his lap. "I'm sorry, sweetheart, but it's one of Austin's dancers," he said, rising. "I'll be back soon, I promise."

The simmering heat still lingering in his gaze warmed her. "I wasn't planning on going anywhere...without you," she added huskily.

His deep, resonant chuckle skirted along her nerve endings. "You hold that thought," he said, hastily rebuttoning his hunter-green shirt as the doorbell chimed yet again. He strolled to the door and stopped, looking over his shoulder at her. "Don't move," he ordered with a sexy smile, then slipped through the door.

A chill brushed her exposed skin and she shivered, not so much from the cold, but from the reality that suddenly slammed into her. The force of it made her realize she had no choice but to leave.

What was she doing? Making love to a man wasn't the problem. Making love to Jordan was an enormous mistake, at least until she sat him down and told him that the Cait Sullivan he'd made fall apart in his arms was an impostor, a fraud and a liar of the first degree. Until she confessed her sins, they'd have no relationship, because anything that happened between them would only be another lie. She had to tell him, and until she did, there could be no more searing kisses, no more tender caresses, and not another, single earth-shattering orgasm. Jordan hadn't even made love to *her*; he'd made love to an illusion.

With more reluctance and regret than she ever believed she was capable of experiencing, she slipped off the window seat, pulled her dress up and struggled with the back zipper. Turning to look for her heels, she caught her reflection in the mirror. The dozens of roses reflected in the triptych weren't the only illusion in the room, she thought with self-disgust.

The slightly swollen lips were real. Her short auburn curls, mussed from Jordan's fingers running through them, haphazardly framed her face. The tiny red mark on her neck stood as testament that what had transpired between them was as real as it got. Too bad it was all under pretense.

Guilt swamped her and she felt like a hypocrite. All along she'd thought Jordan a party to a reprehensible scam, but instead it was *her* pretending to be someone else.

She had to get out of here. When he returned after whatever business he had to attend to with Austin's employee, he couldn't find her sitting upon the window seat like some Victorian courtesan awaiting his pleasure.

Gathering her purse, she sifted through the contents until she found her brush and restored a bit of order to her hair, then applied a fresh coat of lipstick to her kiss-swollen lips. Pausing at the door, she looked around the room one last time. The tapers had burned more than halfway. What was left of the delicious meal he'd prepared lay uneaten upon the pristine white china. Beside her discarded napkin lay the perfect red rose that had so lovingly adorned her plate. Unsure why, she lifted the rose from the table, carefully wrapped it in the napkin and laid it inside her purse before turning to leave.

Her quick escape was halted by the sound of the masculine voices she heard when she reached the bottom of the petal-littered staircase. To her right, in the room off the entryway where she'd first met Jordan only a few days ago, she heard his deep, velvet voice.

A part of her wanted to slink away unnoticed, but she couldn't do anything quite so low. Considering her current track record, that thought was almost laughable, but she still didn't have the nerve to sneak away like a thief in the night.

Summoning the staunch resolve that always saw her through tough situations, and a hefty dose of determination not to buckle if Jordan urged her to stay, she walked into the office—and nearly suffered a coronary arrest.

Travis Michaelson, one of her sister's friends from college, stood near the edge of the desk talking to Jordan as if the two of them were old friends. Travis said something that caused Jordan to laugh. The sound echoed through her shocked mind.

A cold chill ran down her spine and settled in the pit of her stomach when both men turned to look at her. She should have slipped out as she'd seriously contemplated. But no, her conscience wouldn't let her.

Travis gave her a warm, welcoming grin, his deep, brown eyes filled with curiosity. "Cait, what you are doing here?"

She stepped into the room and managed a grin. "Hi, Travis," she said, despite the constricting band tightening her chest.

"You two know each other?" Jordan asked, giving her an odd look.

"Travis and my sister Donna went to college together," she offered in a hurried tone. "I didn't know you worked for Fantasy for Hire," she said to Travis, although the tall, blond Adonis certainly had what it took to fulfill women's fantasies.

"It's not exactly a lifelong ambition for any of us," he answered.

"How many are there?"

"About a dozen, right, Jordan?"

"Fourteen."

"Are you all students?"

Travis nodded. "For the most part. We've got a law student, a couple of budding accountants that I know, and another intern I'm working with at San Francisco General. Unfortunately, med school creates more bills than it pays," he added with a sheepish grin, then turned his attention back to Jordan.

Travis slipped something from his pocket and set it on the desk. "I picked up an extra booking at the Montclair bachelorette party tonight for next month."

"Good work." Jordan opened the envelope, then bent over the desk to write the date on the schedule.

Cait wanted to leave, to run as far away and as fast as possible, but her fear overrode her self-disgust, keeping her feet rooted to the worn carpet. Not only was her story a thing of the past, but she feared Travis might inadvertently say something revealing to Jordan before she had the chance to tell him the truth herself. At least if she stayed, perhaps she could divert any discussion about her for the time being.

"What are you doing here?" Travis asked her, his dark, bedroom eyes filled with idle curiosity.

Play it cool, Sullivan.

"Jordan and I were just...uh...having dinner together," she said, then cast a surreptitious glance in her valentine's direction in time to see a rascal's grin tug his lips.

She crossed the room to the desk, then perched her hip on the ledge, hoping she appeared more nonchalant than she was feeling. Her stomach twisted in knots and her heart thudded almost painfully in her chest.

"Sorry to interrupt," Travis said with a knowing chuckle. "We were just finishing up. Weren't we, Jordan?"

Jordan dropped into the worn leather desk chair and looked up at her, his eyes blazing with sexual intent. "We were just getting started on dessert," he said brazenly.

Her face warmed at his wickedness. "Actually, we're finished," she returned coolly. "I really need to be going. I've got an early appointment. Travis, can I give you a ride?"

The Adonis shook his head. "I've got my pickup, but thanks. Oh, Jordan, before I forget. They gave me a check for that new booking next month." Travis pulled the check from his pocket and handed it to Jordan before turning his attention back to Cait. "I received the invitation for your parents' anniversary party. I doubt I'll be able make it. Jordan's got me pretty busy that night."

"Thanks again for taking that double booking," Jordan said, then slipped a receipt book from the metal tray. Cait absently glanced down when he flipped open the journal.

"I know my parents would be thrilled to see you. Donna would, too, I'm sure."

Something flashed in Travis's eyes, but what it was

all about, Cait couldn't be sure. As far as she knew, Travis and Donna were just friends, but he'd spent many a night in her mother's kitchen with Donna, studying ancient Greek history. She looked down as Jordan filled out a cash receipt for the check Travis had given him, and her breath stopped. Clipped to the top of the page was a receipt to Theodora Spencer in the sum of a thousand dollars for "services rendered."

A loud buzzing, like a telephone left off the hook, filled her mind. Her fingers slipped over the edge of the desk and she gripped it, as she stared at the verification proving Louden Avery's claim.

Her gaze slipped to the schedule spread over the desk. In large, red block letters she read: A & T Hawaii, with a thick line drawn through the week. Someone was lying, and as much as she wanted to believe otherwise, she didn't think it was Avery. He had nothing to loose, whereas Jordan and his brother had a very lucrative business at stake.

How could she deny it when such incriminating evidence lay inches away, condemning Fantasy for Hire as a sex-for-sale operation? Louden had been adamant that the receipt existed, even hinting at the purpose...a week of sun, fun and sex for a price. A part of her had hoped for nothing more than unfounded accusations, but no longer. She'd seen both with her own eyes, and she felt physically ill.

Honeymoon? Is that what they were calling it these days, she thought bitterly.

"How much does the agency usually charge for the standard fantasy?" she asked Jordan. Her voice sounded far away, as though she was in a dark tunnel and the pinpoint of light at the end was quickly fading.

Jordan tore off the receipt and handed it to Travis. "Two hundred," he said, effectively dousing the light and leaving her in total darkness. "Why?" he asked.

Cait shrugged. "Just curious. What's your take, Travis?"

Travis stuffed the receipt in the front pocket of the dark red T-shirt that hugged his massive chest. "Austin pays us about forty percent of whatever we make, plus an extra ten on any bookings we happen to bring in ourselves. Not bad for about half an hour's work. Some nights I'll get a couple of bookings, which is a big help for us starving-student types."

She nodded slowly. "Yeah, a real big help," she murmured. She slid off the desk, surprised her legs held her. "I really need to be going," she said abruptly. "Good night."

"Cait, wait," Jordan called as she reached the doorway.

She heard the squeak of the chair, but kept walking, hoping he wouldn't follow her. She couldn't bear to look at him. Not when her heart was shattering into a million tiny pieces. "I'll see you tomorrow," she muttered, then hurried out the door before anyone could stop her.

Somehow, she made it down the steps, crushing the rose petals that had led her to what she'd foolishly believed had been real rather than make-believe. When she reached her car, she started the engine and drove away without turning back. Blessed numbness settled over her, which was a good thing, she figured, since she didn't know if she could withstand the pain of her breaking heart.

He'd lied to her. Lied to her about everything.

Tonight had been real, he'd said. As real as it got.

For whom? she wondered bitterly as she came to a stop at a traffic signal. For her, and the money she'd paid him to pretend what was happening between them was real? Or for him? The standard price for a fantasy was two hundred dollars. She'd paid him ten times that and demanded the works. Well, she'd certainly gotten her money's worth.

Although she'd done nothing but lie to Jordan herself since they'd met, she still hurt. She still didn't know when she'd lost her perspective, but she had. The story had somehow become less and less important as her feelings for Jordan had changed.

And that had been her biggest mistake.

She'd paid him to sweep her off her feet, and he had.

She'd paid him to make her come apart in his arms. He hadn't disappointed her on that score, either.

She'd wanted to learn the truth behind the agency and, Lord, had she ever. She'd covered enough charity functions to recognize the Spencer name as one of San Francisco's finest families. When Theodora Spencer had broken her engagement to Bartholomew What's-His-Name, it had made the society pages. She knew because one of her stories had been bumped in favor of the broken Spencer engagement. If she remembered correctly, Ms. Spencer had worked as a graphic designer.

Theodora Spencer was the woman who had worked for Louden Avery, the one who had paid

Fantasy for Hire for sex. Now that she'd seen the incriminating evidence herself, she had no choice but to continue as planned.

Twenty minutes later, she pulled Brian's Lexus into the garage and entered the house. The enormous Pacific Heights home was quiet, as it always was, but she welcomed the silence. The solitude would allow her the vital time she needed to form her next plan of action. And to wallow in some much-needed self-pity.

She walked into the den and spied her laptop on the desk, sitting next to the vase filled with an array of flowers that started with the letter C. She pulled the rose from her purse and stalked to the desk. Grabbing the flowers in both hands, she angrily tossed them into the wastebasket.

"That's what you get for thinking for a minute he was the real thing," she chastised herself.

Her throat constricted with tears. Hadn't her mother always told her children to be careful what they wished for—because they just might get it? "Right again, Mom," she muttered, pulling out the chair. She plopped down and folded her arms on the gleaming wood.

The phone rang, but she ignored it. She didn't want to talk to anyone. Not Jen, who'd wisely warned her she was going to get hurt, nor her sisters, each of whom would know in a second she was upset about something.

The machine clicked on and she heard her voice telling the caller to leave a message, followed by a long, steady beep. "Cait, it's Jordan." She closed her eyes. "Cait, if you're there, pick up the phone."

Her eyes burned with tears she struggled not to shed. Tonight had been one of the most beautiful of her life, but it had all been shattered when she'd finally seen the proof she needed to go forward with the story. She might have led Jordan to believe she was cool and sophisticated, but the truth was far different. The truth was, she'd fallen in love with the lying cad. He'd been everything Louden had claimed. He might not have been the one to take the money from Theodora Spencer in exchange for sex, but he'd taken *her* money, and gone above and beyond on the damned seduction clause of their agreement.

She considered reaching for the phone to tell him what she really thought, until his next words stopped her. "We need to talk, Cait. Call me."

Had Travis told him about her? Did he already know she'd been lying all along, too?

There was a bit of irony she hadn't expected. Obviously they were made for each other—because they were both claiming to be something they weren't.

JORDAN SLAMMED DOWN the receiver in frustration. For the past two hours, he'd called Cait every thirty minutes. The only conversation he'd had was one-sided, with her answering machine.

He'd thought everything between them settled. He'd been convinced that after tonight, there'd be no more questions about whether or not what they'd both been fighting all week was a losing battle of mutual attraction. Oh sure, he still had questions about her, but he'd concluded he had the rest of his life to find out all of her little idiosyncrasies and nuances.

Until she'd given him a look that had chilled him to

the bone when she'd left. She'd looked at him as if he'd held no more value than a moldy container of food left in the refrigerator for so long it was unrecognizable.

And then he'd gotten ticked off.

So what if he was being unreasonable? he thought grumpily. As far as he knew, he'd done nothing to warrant the icy chill or the look of contempt she'd tossed his way before running out on him. He didn't have a clue what had gone wrong, and he wasn't about to let her get away from him without an explanation.

By the time he pulled up the slope of Cait's driveway twenty minutes later, his rising irritation hadn't ebbed. Not even the climb up the brick steps he'd taken two at a time to her front door, nor the chilled sea air, helped to lessen his rapidly mounting frustration. He rang the bell, and waited.

When she opened the door, he stalked past her into the elegant foyer without waiting for an invitation, then turned to face her. With his hands planted firmly on his hips, he raked his gaze over her. Gone was the sophisticated woman who'd turned him inside out with need only a few hours ago. A pair of faded jeans, ripped at the knee, and a gray, faded UC–San Francisco sweatshirt replaced the black slip of a dress. Her face, scrubbed clean of makeup, made her look about eighteen.

And completely adorable.

Damn if she didn't fire his blood, even if he was ticked at her for running out on him and making him think *he'd* done something wrong. "Why'd you leave like that?" he demanded.

She crossed her arms and cocked an eyebrow. "I told you," she started, her voice the epitome of calm, cool and controlled. "I have an early appointment in the morning. I didn't know our business arrangement entitled you to my personal schedule." She snapped her fingers. "I must have missed that clause in the contract."

He narrowed his eyes at her sarcasm. "Don't get smart with me, Cait," he warned. "I want to know what the hell is going on here. Why'd you run out as if you couldn't stand to be in the same room with me for another minute?"

With a toss of her curls, she strode past him. "It's not important."

God, he hated when women said that. There should be a law against it, because whatever they claimed as unimportant, always was *extremely* important. At least to them.

He followed her into the den. "Sorry, sweetheart," he said as she plopped down on the sofa facing the fire crackling in the hearth. "I'm not buying that one."

"I don't expect you to," she said, her fiery green gaze colliding with his. "After all, you are in the business of selling."

He didn't like the tone of her voice, or the look of disgust in her eyes. "What are you trying to say?"

She blew out a stream of breath that ruffled her auburn bangs and stood. "Nothing, Jordan," she said, her voice filled with something he didn't comprehend. "I paid you, quite handsomely I might add, for a service, which you've provided. In fact, I'd say you've gone above and beyond the norm."

"Meaning?" he prompted, having a good idea where she was headed.

"The standard price for a fantasy is two hundred dollars. I paid you ten times that amount. It only makes sense that you'd—" the crease in her forehead deepened "—go above and beyond the call of duty."

"You're the one who asked for the works."

She circled the square cocktail table and crossed the room to the fireplace. "True," she said, opening the grate. She bent over to toss another log onto the fire. Just the sight of her denim-covered, curvy backside had his temperature climbing a notch or two.

She straightened and turned, pinning him with an angry look. "And you certainly gave me the works tonight, didn't you?" She laughed, but the sound was more self-deprecating than humorous. "I should have left you a gratuity, because you were good. Very good. I don't know any other man who would have been quite so *unselfish*."

He forgot about her curvy bottom and concentrated on her words instead. In two long strides, he was standing in front of her, unsure what to say to get through to her. "Tonight wasn't part of the 'service,' Cait. Tonight it was you and me. Two people who..."

"Who what, Jordan? Have a contract?"

"No," he retorted, frustration making his voice harsh. How dare she cheapen what had happened tonight. Earlier, he'd cursed the interruption of the doorbell. Now he was grateful, because he'd been right about waiting until her fantasy was complete before pursuing any type of personal relationship with her. "Tonight was about two people who care about each other."

He caught a glimpse of pain in her eyes, but then it was gone, replaced by the icy coldness he'd seen earlier in Austin's office. "It was just a part of the service you provided."

"The hell it was," he shot at her irritably. She stepped away, but he caught hold of her arm and pulled her against him. "You're wrong, Cait," he said, sliding his hands down her slender back to cup her bottom. "It was only the two of us in that room tonight. No agreements. No services rendered. Just you and me, sweetheart. And this," he added before swooping down to capture her mouth in a searing kiss meant to show her exactly how he felt about her.

She didn't struggle; she issued one of those soft, little moans that heightened his awareness to the point of pain, before slipping her arms around his neck. He had no trouble mistaking her response as need, a need that matched his own. Damn. What was it about her that turned him inside out and had him wanting to make love to her every chance he got?

He kissed her slowly and thoroughly, so she'd have no doubt that he was kissing her because he wanted her, and not as part of some stupid agreement. She pressed her delicious little body against his when his hand made caressing sweeps down the length of her spine. She returned the kiss, her mouth going all hot and soft with the promise of sensual delights even his imagination had a hard time cataloging.

God, he wanted her. Wanted her like he'd never wanted another woman.

He ended the kiss to search her face. The coldness in her eyes had faded and he saw the first stirring of heat sparking her gaze, salving his wounded male pride.

"How can you deny this is as real as it gets?" he asked, gently cupping her face in both palms. He stroked his thumb over the pulse beating wildly at her temple. "I dare you to deny this is real," he said, then caught her mouth again with his to cajole her tongue to mate with his.

By the time he finally lifted his head to look into her eyes again, hers were heavy lidded and passion-filled. "It's just a fantasy," she whispered quietly. "A fantasy I paid you to create."

He let her go and shoved his hand through his hair in frustration. He had to find a way to make her believe it was her he wanted and not her damned money. Without a word, he stepped around her to the desk. Reaching into his hip pocket, he withdrew his checkbook and wrote her a check in the amount of two thousand dollars. When he finished, he slammed the check down on the desk, a spark of satisfaction coursing through him when she flinched.

He strode to the door, but her voice stopped him.

"Jordan, I..."

"The next time I kiss you," he said, angrily yanking open the door, "there should be no doubt in your mind it's me and not some damned obligation."

10

CAIT PLUCKED a chunk of blue cheese from her Cobb salad and set it on the pristine-white plate, listening halfheartedly to Sharon's complaint about the hotel caterer unable to deliver their father's favorite grape leaves.

"We're doing beef wonton instead," Cait said, frowning when she bit into a piece of hard-boiled egg she'd missed on her first pass through the salad. "Dad loves those, too."

"Why do you order that salad?" Linda asked her before taking a sip of iced tea. "You always pick out half the ingredients."

"Because I like the way they chop the lettuce," Cait said, finding another chunk of blue cheese. To Donna, she said, "I saw Travis Michaelson the other night."

Donna's pale green eyes lit up with interest. "Really? Where?"

Now she'd done it, wondering how she could get out of answering the more personal questions her sisters were bound to ask. No, they wouldn't ask, she thought. They would cross-examine. "I was having dinner with...a friend, and he happened to stop by. He told me he can't make it to the party tonight."

"Who's the friend?" Sharon, the only blue-eyed Sullivan of the bunch, asked. The four of them might carry the Sullivan name, but there was no denying any of them their Murphy heritage. Hair of varying shades of red along with pale, creamy complexions marked them all Margaret Murphy Sullivan's daughters, along with quick tongues and equally quick senses of humor.

Although thankful she was no longer complaining about the caterer, Cait wished her sister would latch on to some other new subject. She gave her sister a cheeky grin she really wasn't feeling. "You'll meet him tonight."

"The one who sent the flowers?" Linda asked.

"Flowers?" Sharon added pepper to her tuna salad. "Who sent our Caitie flowers?"

"It was nothing," Cait said, ignoring the curious expressions lighting her sisters' faces.

Linda laughed and shook her head. "Don't let her fool you. Brian's dining-room table was completely covered with flowers and plants."

Only the most beautiful things begin with the letter C.

Had that been real? Cait wondered. She no longer knew what was real and what had been a part of the fantasy.

"Caitie, are you keeping things from me?" Sharon asked with a lift of her strawberry-blond eyebrows.

"Stop acting like a mother," she told Sharon.

"I am a mother, so I can get away with it."

"I think it sounds like a serious relationship," Donna said.

"Butt out," Cait warned, pointing her fork threateningly at each of her sisters. "I want each one of you to promise me you'll butt out."

"It is definitely serious," Sharon said to Donna with a wide grin.

"It is not," Cait retorted, but her argument lacked conviction. That was her problem. Whenever she thought of Jordan, she had some very serious thoughts.

"Oh, come on, Caitie," Donna laughed and flicked her thick auburn braid over her slender shoulder. "You've never been a good liar."

Her sisters would be surprised if they knew just how adept she'd become in that very role this past week.

"What does he do for a living?" Sharon asked.

Cait sighed. There was no hope. "He's an architect."

"Ooh, a professional man."

Donna leaned forward and grinned. "What's he look like?"

"A cross between the Frankenstein monster and Broomhilda."

"What's got you in such a snit, Caitie?" Donna reached across the table for the basket of warmed sourdough.

"Nothing," she said sulkily. "I've got work to do, is all." Another lie, she thought. All she'd done last night and this morning was stare at the blank computer screen with her chin propped in one hand while the fingers of her free hand drummed the gleaming surface of the desk top. She couldn't have written two words if her life depended on it, let alone string coherent sentences together.

Her story was slowly slipping away from her. With her own eyes she'd seen the evidence, yet she still couldn't bring herself to write the exposé. She continually came up with excuse after excuse as to why she couldn't go forward as she'd originally planned. She needed more, like verification of the verification. So what if Theodora Spencer had paid a grand for a week-long getaway fantasy? She probably had a very good reason. And without confirming the details with Ms. Spencer herself, she couldn't expose the paper to the kind of lawsuits that could be brought against it. A thousand dollars for a fantasy didn't go very far to confirm Avery's claims of illicit shenanigans at Fantasy for Hire. Nor were a series of lawsuits exactly the way to catapult a career, she thought with a sigh of disgust.

Maybe there was another reason Louden Avery was so intent on her exposing Fantasy for Hire and/or Theodora Spencer. Maybe he was a jilted lover who wanted to cause trouble for his ex. What could cause a better scandal than linking one of San Francisco's most prominent families to an agency specializing in sensual fantasies?

With a sigh, she pulled another piece of boiled egg from her salad, nodding absently at something Donna said about the decorations. Lord, she was so confused. She'd give anything to recapture the excitement she'd felt a week ago about her scoop, but with every moment she'd spent in Jordan's company, her enthusiasm for the story had waned. She tried to find solace in the fact that she might still have a story. After all, she'd paid him a hefty sum for the works, and had received the full service.

Except Jordan had given back the money she'd paid him.

She didn't want to think about the harsh look on his face, but she couldn't seem to get that, or his parting words, out of her mind. *The next time I kiss you...*

After the way she'd behaved, she was surprised he was even considering a next time.

"...meet him tonight. Right, Caitie?"

Cait looked at Linda. "What did you say?"

Linda sighed, a sound of great exasperation. "I said, Mom's going to be thrilled to finally meet your mystery man tonight."

"Oh my God," she gasped. "I forgot about Mom." Cait closed her eyes and dropped her head in her hands. "She'll blow my cover. What am I going to do?"

"Cover?" Linda asked.

"What are you talking about?" Sharon demanded.

"Blow what?" Donna added to the mix.

As much as Cait didn't want to tell her sisters about Jordan, she realized she had no choice, especially if she was going to keep up the pretense just a while longer. Until she told Jordan the truth about who she really was, she couldn't take the risk of him discovering the only debutante balls she'd ever attended were the ones she'd reported on for the newspaper.

She lifted her gaze and the concern in their eyes warmed her. Her sisters might be a bunch of busybodies, but they loved her and would do just about anything for her. As much as she complained about them, she also knew they'd always be there for her when she needed them. And as much as she dreaded telling them everything she'd been up to lately, and no doubt hearing a series of lectures from each of them, at least she knew they cared.

"I need your help," she said quietly. "I need you to run interference for me tonight. Jordan can't know that I'm a reporter."

Sharon paused, the butter knife held over her half-buttered sourdough bread. "Who does he think you are?"

"Not who," Cait admitted, embarrassed. "What."

"Okay then, *what* does he think you are?" Donna asked.

"Rich. Disgustingly rich."

She expected lectures. She even expected a few condolences for screwing up what could have been the first very serious relationship of her adult life. The last thing she expected were gales of laughter. "It's not funny."

"Caitie, what on earth possessed you to do such a thing?" Sharon asked between giggles.

With a great deal of reluctance, she spent the next thirty minutes explaining nearly everything, from the moment Louden Avery tossed in her lap what she'd believed had been the story of her career, to Jordan giving her back her money, leaving out only the most intimate details. By the time they inspected the ballroom and headed to the parking lot an hour later, her sisters were as sympathetic as she'd hoped.

Sharon slung her arm over Cait's shoulders as they stopped by Linda's car. "Mom's the only one we have to worry about. She's so proud of you, and won't miss an opportunity to brag about her 'Little Caitie Bug' to anyone who will listen."

Cait groaned at her mother's nickname for her. Not exactly the kind of name a debutante would proudly carry, she thought with a self-deprecating grin.

"When are you going to tell Mr. Valentine the truth?" Linda asked, always the older and wiser sister, according to Linda.

"Tonight, after the party. I'm not writing the story," she admitted, surprised by the sense of freedom she felt voicing that statement. "I'll tell him everything then."

Sharon's arm tightened around her. "Good luck, Caitie Bug. I think you're going to need it," she said sympathetically.

She gave her sister a weak grin. "Thanks." She would need it, because no matter how she played the scenario in her mind, it always ended the same...with a broken heart when Jordan told her he never wanted to see her again.

JORDAN BRACED his arm on the windowsill above his head and stared out at the backyard. The leaves of the avocado tree he and Austin had climbed as kids needed to be raked, and the shrubs lining the cinder block were due for a trim. He considered heading outside for some good old-fashioned manual labor, but he had a party to dress for in another couple of hours. Besides, he doubted the physical labor would get his mind off Cait.

He hadn't spoken to her since he'd stormed out of her place, but then again, he hadn't really expected to since she'd called and left a message telling him she wouldn't be able to keep their date Friday night. Her tone had been cool and businesslike, and hadn't done much to ease his frustration.

"Jordan? This just arrived for you."

He turned at the sound of his sister-in-law's voice

and smiled. Austin and Teddy had returned from their honeymoon only a few hours ago and already he was feeling out of place in his own home. He'd gone to look at some real-estate possibilities, but found that he'd wanted Cait's opinion before he made a final decision. That thought irritated him more than her all-business attitude when she'd called. He tried telling himself he didn't need Cait's opinion, or even want her approval, but knew he was lying to himself. He wanted her approval for the simple reason he hoped she'd be spending most of her time at his new place.

He took the manila envelope from Teddy and opened it. Inside was the contract awarding him the bid on the strip malls. He'd received the call from the developer the previous afternoon with a promise to overnight the contract to him. All he had to do was sign it and he'd be on his way to building Advanced Architectural Designs into the self-supporting business he'd been dreaming of for far too long.

He tossed the contracts on the counter.

Teddy's dark brown eyes filled with concern. "Austin and I were going to order a pizza," she said, crossing the kitchen to the sink. "Will you join us?"

"Thanks, but no," he said, shoving his hands into the pockets of his trousers. "I've got...an appointment." He frowned. Now _he_ was starting to sound like Cait.

Austin sauntered into the kitchen and patted his wife's behind on his way to the refrigerator.

"If you're sure," Teddy said, a sweet smile tugging her lips.

"I'm sure."

"Sure about what?" Austin asked, poking his dark head into the refrigerator.

Teddy rinsed the glass that was sitting on the counter and placed it in the dishwasher. "Jordan's going out tonight. I think he has a date," she added in a bad stage whisper.

Austin's eyebrows rose and curiosity filled his green eyes. "What? With a woman? You mean to tell me my big brother's finally dragging himself away from his dollhouses to play with a real doll?"

"They're architectural models," Jordan said with a frown. His little brother may be all grown up, but that didn't mean Jordan still couldn't give Austin that stern look he'd learned to perfect when they were kids. "And you didn't complain when they helped pay your way through college."

"*Helped* is the operative word," Austin retorted good-naturedly. "Fantasy for Hire paid off my student loans and gave me enough capital to get Mc-Bride Commercial Landscaping off the ground. So, who's the woman?"

"I'll leave you two boys alone," Teddy said with a lighthearted laugh. "I'm going to finish unpacking."

The look Austin gave his new bride was filled with love and affection, something Jordan was beginning to understand all too well. He just wished he knew what he was going to do next.

Austin pulled out a bar stool and sat. "So, who is she?" he asked again, reaching into a brass colander for a fresh pear.

Jordan sat and pulled the contract in front of him. At least now he had viable employment, even if it didn't do much by way of putting him on equal financial footing with Cait. "You wouldn't know her," he said, scanning the standardized contract.

"Uh-oh," Austin said between bites of pear. "Is it serious?"

Jordan sighed and pushed the contract aside to read later when he was in a better frame of mind. Right now, all he could think about was a particular redhead intent on twisting him up in knots. "It could be."

Austin chuckled. "Trouble in paradise, huh?"

"She's...stubborn."

"I know all about stubborn," Austin said, leaning back and looking toward the living room where Teddy was bent over the contents of a packing carton.

"I heard that," Teddy called from the other room.

Austin's chuckle deepened. "How do they do that?" he asked rhetorically with a shake of his head.

Teddy reentered the kitchen and gave her husband a tolerant look before slipping up behind him to wrap her arms around his neck. "It's a woman thing," she said, her sleek blond hair falling over Austin's shoulder. Looking up at Jordan, she repeated her husband's question, "Who is she?"

Jordan thought for a moment, and was stunned to realize he didn't know. All he knew about Cait Sullivan was that he wanted her, not that he'd tell that to his sister-in-law and brother. "Maybe you know her. Her family's well connected. Cait Sullivan?"

Teddy's forehead creased. "Doesn't ring a bell, Jordan. Sorry. How'd you meet her?"

A smile tugged his lips. "She was looking for a fantasy."

Austin laughed. "There's something to be said

about a woman with a fantasy," he said, slipping his hand over Teddy's.

"By the way, you owe me two grand," Jordan said, rising.

Austin's eyebrows pulled together in a frown. "What for?" he demanded.

"I reimbursed Cait. I gave her back the money she paid me."

Teddy's eyebrows rose and she grinned, while confusion clouded his brother's eyes.

"Jordan, I've never charged two grand for a fantasy," Austin said, his voice incredulous.

Jordan looked from Teddy to Austin and back again. "What about...?"

Teddy's grin widened and a becoming blush stained her cheeks. "That was a special circumstance," she offered. "I was feeling a little...desperate at the time."

Desperate was not an adjective Jordan would ever apply to Cait. Determined, like when she'd hired him to be her valentine and wouldn't take no for an answer. "What *do* you charge when someone asks for the works?" he asked, his confusion mounting.

"The works?" Austin's frown deepened. "There is no 'works.' Standard services, Jordan. Birthdays, bachelorette parties or whatever, but all the guys do is dance, reek charm and hope to get another booking. They leave a gift with a business card before going on to the next appointment. End of story. What did you do to my business?"

"You should have told me more about it before taking off," Jordan complained, but returned to the bar stool and sat. By the time he finished explaining in detail his association with Cait, he'd left little doubt in the newlyweds' minds that he was damned serious about turning fantasy into reality with Cait Sullivan.

Austin shook his head in disbelief, a lock of dark hair falling over his forehead. "What are you going to do now, Mr. Valentine?" his brother teased.

"I'm not sure," Jordan admitted. "There's no longer a contractual obligation standing between us. Tonight, it's going to be just the two of us."

A situation he had every intention of taking advantage of, although he knew next to nothing about her. A problem he planned on solving, even if it meant spending the rest of his life doing it.

"DON'T PARK in there."

Jordan glanced over at Cait. Her face, illuminated by the lights of the dashboard of his 4X4, was dead serious. "This is the hotel, right?"

"Yes, but there's free parking a block and half down," she said, pointing in that direction.

"Sweetheart, it's supposed to rain."

"It won't," she said, still indicating the free parking sign down the street. "It wouldn't dare rain tonight."

"Don't hold your breath about Mother Nature cooperating, Cait," he said, then turned into the hotel's parking garage despite her complaint about paying for overpriced parking.

"In the one-hundred-plus-years history of the Rose Parade, it's never rained on the actual day of the parade. Tonight is my parents' fortieth anniversary. I'll accept nothing less for them, so park down the block."

"You sure about that?" he teased.

"Absolutely. It doesn't make any sense to pay for something when it's free."

"I'll pay because I don't want to walk two blocks in the rain," he said, pulling up to the attendant's booth to retrieve the parking ticket, writing off her odd behavior as another one of those little idiosyncrasies he was determined to discover one by one.

He pulled into an available slot and killed the engine. Her hand reached for the door handle, but he stopped her. She turned to look at him, her green eyes filled with curiosity. He reached toward her, trailing the back of his hand down her silky cheek. "You look beautiful tonight."

Even in the dim lights of the parking garage he could see a slight blush darken her skin. "Thank you," she whispered. A saucy grin tugged her lips. "And you look every inch the fantasy."

He cupped his hand behind her neck and gently eased her toward him. "This isn't a fantasy, sweetheart. *This*," he said, lips hovering a breath away, "is reality."

Her eyes darkened, and her lips parted. He accepted her invitation, sliding his tongue inside the sweet cavern of her mouth to collect her unique flavor. He caught a tiny, delicate moan as her hand smoothed over his shoulder, her fingers curling into the hair at the nape of his neck.

It took every ounce of willpower he possessed to end the kiss when all he could think about was taking her home and making love to her. "Any doubts about who was kissing you?" he asked with a lift to his eyebrow.

Her smile was brief and something flashed in her eyes he didn't quite understand. "None."

"Good," he said with a firm nod, then slipped from the truck. He opened her door, and she turned, her wool coat falling open to reveal the legs responsible for inspiring his imagination. She wore stockings again, and he couldn't help being more than a little disappointed they weren't the black ones held up by those little red satin bows that made him crazy. As she slid from the truck, his gaze traveled up to the hem of a short, off-white velvet dress that hugged her curves. She moved to step around him, but he grabbed her hand in his and pulled her toward him.

With one hand, he closed the door, while he used the other to hold her against him. "You're making me nuts, woman," he growled, dipping his head to nuzzle her ear.

"We really should be getting inside," she said, but wreathed her arms around his neck and pressed against him instead.

"Shh," he murmured as her mouth sought his.

Heat flared instantly between them, as it had been doing all week, but now he didn't have their stupid agreement hanging over their heads. Tonight, he planned to make her his in every sense of the word. And from her response, he didn't doubt for a minute she wanted the same.

He ended the kiss far too soon, but she was right. They did have to get inside and he didn't think she'd appreciate her family knowing they'd been in the parking garage groping each other like a couple of teenagers. "I want to know you, Cait. I want to know everything about you."

The heat in her eyes dimmed and she looked away. "We should get inside. My sisters will be waiting for me."

Concern nipped at him. He lifted his hand and cupped her warm cheek in his palm. She turned toward the heat, closing her eyes. "What's wrong, Cait?"

She looked up at him. The same concern rippling through him creased her forehead and filled her eyes. "Nothing," she said, flashing him a bright smile that didn't decrease the worry in her gaze. "Tonight's just important to me, is all. It's a big night for my parents and I want everything to be perfect for them."

"It will be," he said, taking her hand in his and bringing her chilled fingers to his lips.

A wistful expression crossed her face as she looked into his eyes. "There's something I need to tell you. I'm not who you think I am."

"You're the woman I want. That's all I need to know."

She shook her head. "No, I mean—"

He kissed her again, short and quick, but that didn't lessen the flare of heat rising inside him again. He slid his hand into her hair and used his thumb to trace the lobe of her ear. "We have the rest of our lives to learn everything about each other," he said quietly.

"I wish I could believe that," she answered cryptically.

"Believe it, sweetheart," he said, pulling her against him in hopes of chasing away whatever demons rode with her tonight. Her arms slipped around his waist and she rested her head against his chest.

He breathed in her scent and smiled. "I don't ever want to let you go. You're important to me, Cait."

More than important, he thought. As with his brother, fantasy had become reality. And in this reality the rules were different and forever took on a whole new meaning.

Whether he'd wanted it to happen or not, somehow he'd fallen in love with a very confusing, extremely frustrating, but beautiful redhead he knew next to nothing about.

11

SHE'D TRIED. She'd really tried to tell him, but he'd said it didn't matter. God, if only she could believe that, but she was afraid to hope.

"Jordan, would you like another piece of cake?" Margaret Sullivan asked from behind them, a plate filled with a slice of anniversary cake in her hands.

Jordan turned and gave her mother one of those charming smiles he'd been gracing her sisters and cousins with all evening, effectively wrapping every female within a two-foot radius effortlessly around his finger. "No, thank you," he answered, patting his stomach with a chuckle. "I couldn't eat another bite."

Cait hid a grin behind her champagne flute when her mother shook her head and sat, that look she'd perfected over the years that said she didn't believe him for a moment gracing her still-beautiful face.

"Are you sure you've had enough to eat?" Margaret asked, her voice filled with concern. "If you wait for any of my daughters to feed you, you'll starve. I know how these career girls are—always working and too busy to spend time in the kitchen to prepare a proper meal."

The champagne lodged in Cait's throat and burned before sliding down her throat to ignite a bonfire in her stomach. Cait coughed and stood abruptly.

"We're fine, Mom," she said quickly, too quickly, but she couldn't help herself. Panic did that to a person.

Ignoring her mother's frown, Cait tossed her napkin on the table. "The deejay's about to get started. Jordan, do you want to dance?" she asked hurriedly, desperate to get him away from her mother before her rapidly crumbling cover was completely blown.

"Wouldn't it be better to wait for the music to start?" he asked, his voice tinged with amusement.

She frowned and bit her lip. "You're right."

Oh God, what was she going to do? Where were her sisters when she needed them? She looked frantically around the ballroom and found them at another table laughing and having a grand time. "Let's go see what the holdup is," she suggested.

"Caitie Bug, sit down," her mother chided, the touch of Irish in her voice revealing that stubborn determination Cait knew from experience she'd have little success fighting. "I'd like to chat with your young man."

"Mom, really," she complained, but sat anyway. No one argued with Margaret Sullivan. Her children weren't that foolish. "You don't need to grill Jordan."

"Cait, it's all right," he said, turning up the wattage on that charming smile.

No, it's not! she wanted to shout. *She's going to ruin everything before I have a chance to explain.* Instead, she grabbed her champagne glass and drained it.

"How did you and my Caitie Bug meet?" Margaret asked him, her clear gaze sharp and intent. Her mother's question may have been couched in a conversational tone, but Cait knew her mother all too well. The woman never did anything without a purpose. Just her luck, her purpose now was to give Jordan the good old-fashioned third degree.

"Through a friend," Cait answered before Jordan had a chance to respond. She sent a heated glare in her sisters' direction. The traitors ignored her.

"Have you been dating long?"

"Mom—"

"Only about a week, Mrs. Sullivan," Jordan answered.

"What do you do for a living?"

Cait's eyes rounded at her mother's pointed, and far too personal, question. Her heart beat heavily in her chest as her nightmare continued to spin out of control.

"Mom, I don't—"

Jordan slipped his hand over hers to silence her. "I'm an architect."

"I've always loved architecture," Margaret said with a warm smile. "Have I seen any of your buildings around the city?"

"Mother!" Cait exclaimed. Good grief, why didn't she just ask to see his bank statement?

"Not in the Bay Area, but you will soon. I was just awarded a fairly lucrative contract."

"Congratulations." Margaret smiled.

Cait frowned. "You were?"

Jordan laced their fingers together. "I won the bid on those strip malls. I'll be pretty busy for the next few months."

"But that's a good thing, right?" she asked. At least one of them was lucky enough to see their dreams coming true. She'd be writing fluff for the rest of her life.

"Yeah, but now I've got to find office space, buy more equipment, hire a small staff, plus secure more bids to keep the business going while I'm dealing with all the meetings involved with the developers on my other projects. And now that Austin and Teddy are home from their honeymoon, I really need to find my own place."

Margaret smoothed her hand over the rose-colored dress she'd picked out with Linda earlier that week. "You have family, Jordan?"

"A brother," he said, turning his attention back to Margaret. "And now a sister," he added, his smile telling of the affection he felt for his brother and sister-in-law.

Margaret waved at someone across the room. "My brother-in-law is signaling for me. We'll talk again soon," she added, resting her hand momentarily on Jordan's shoulder before crossing the ballroom.

Cait let out a rush of breath, grateful the immediate danger had passed.

Jordan's grip on her hand tightened slightly. "I like your family," he said.

She couldn't help the smile that instantly tugged her lips despite the close call. "They like you, too." She narrowed her eyes. "Especially my niece, you charmer."

He laughed, the sound warm and intimate. He leaned close, his eyes filled with mischief. "What are my chances of charming her aunt?"

Beneath the warmth of that smile, she forgot about lies and fantasies, concentrating instead on the promise of pleasure. "I'd have to say probably very good."

He looked past her, then back down, his hazel eyes

filled with enough heat to scorch them both. "Can we get out of here?"

All week she'd flirted outrageously with him, doing everything in her small repertoire of seduction skills to leave him with little doubt that she wanted him. Her goal had been to garner a proposition from him, and he'd finally complied.

Although she may have ventured into Fantasy for Hire to discover the reality behind the fantasies, the only thing she'd learned was that she'd ended up falling hard for her valentine. He made her feel things she'd never experienced. He'd charmed her, romanced her and she'd been powerless to prevent her feelings for him from growing into something special, something that had the ability to last a lifetime.

Just her luck, she thought with a halfhearted grin. Now that she had no story, the man finally propositions her.

Her options were limited. She could either tell him the truth now and take the risk of never seeing him again, or she could continue with the fantasy.

"There's something I need to tell you," she said, taking the only available option that had the slightest chance of ensuring her forever with her own special valentine fantasy.

He shifted in his chair and lifted her hand to his lips. "You don't have to say anything, sweetheart. I already know."

Delightful little tingles shot up her arm when he brushed his lips across the back of her hand. "You do?" she managed in a hushed whisper because her voice had suddenly taken flight.

He nodded slowly, and she shivered. "Because I feel the same way."

Her stomach bottomed out and her head spun. If she didn't know better, she'd have sworn he was telling her he loved her. But that was impossible, she thought. He didn't know a thing about her, and what he did know was based on one fabrication after another.

"How did your house hunting go yesterday?" she asked suddenly, anxious to change the subject. She ignored his questioning frown and flashed him a bright, nervous smile.

"I found a couple of prospects," he said as if choosing his words carefully. "Care to offer your opinion?"

Her nervousness increased rather than decreased. "Why would you want my opinion?"

He gave her hand a gentle squeeze. "Because I'm hoping you'll be spending a lot of time there."

With every ounce of self-control she possessed, she forced herself not to close her eyes and issue a painful wail for what she was going to lose the minute he learned the truth. "You do?"

"Cait, don't you get it? We may have met because you wanted to fulfill a fantasy, but that doesn't mean we can't have a lasting relationship. I want to get to know all about you. And I don't care if it takes the rest of our lives for me to do it."

"But—"

"Look, I know we didn't meet under the most ideal circumstances, but neither did Austin and Teddy. She was one of Austin's clients."

She couldn't believe what she was hearing. "No

way," she said, pulling her hand from his. "You're kidding, right?"

He laughed and shook his head. "Theodora Spencer McBride might have paid my brother to be her fantasy date, but the fact remains they fell in love and are now happily married."

Her gaze snapped to his. "Theodora Spencer?" Something wasn't right, but she had a feeling it had nothing to do with the allegations against Fantasy for Hire as she'd been led to believe. Oh no, she thought with a flash of temper for being so gullible. Something wasn't right, and it had everything to do with Louden Avery.

"Do you know Teddy?"

"I know of her," she said, frowning. "But I never heard anything about a Spencer marriage, and believe me, people like the Spencers don't do anything without it being reported in the society columns."

"Probably because they eloped."

She couldn't believe it. All this time she'd been chasing a story that didn't even exist. When she thought of the harm a story like the one she'd been planning could have done to Jordan's brother and new bride, she felt ill.

The music started, a romantic ballad from her parents' heyday. "Let's dance," she said, standing, mentally ticking off twelve different varieties of the fool she'd been, not to mention a coward for not telling Jordan the truth. The evening was still young, she quickly rationalized. She'd tell him later. And she *would*. She didn't have a choice if she hoped to develop any kind of lasting relationship with Jordan McBride, fantasy-come-true.

"Whatever the lady wants," he said, following her to the quickly filling dance floor and pulling her into his arms. He kept their linked hands between them, their fingers laced together intimately.

"Whatever I want," she mused aloud, slipping her free hand over the silk of his navy suit jacket, to slide her fingers through the rich sable hair brushing his collar. "That could be very interesting."

His hand pressed against her lower back, bringing them closer together. "Interesting? It's a start," he said, pressing his lips against hers in a brief, but no less intimate, kiss. "But I'd rather finish what we started the other night."

"You realize if my father sees you kissing me," she said, forcing a casual, disinterested grin in spite of the flare of desire making her feel achy and tight inside at the intimate reminder, "he's going to demand to know your intentions, Mr. McBride."

The teasing light in his eyes belied the frown tugging his eyebrows. "Then I guess I'll have to be more careful in the future and kiss you in more private places."

Her senses overloaded and her imagination needed little prompting. "Ah, then I take it your intentions are anything but honorable?"

"Quite lascivious," he quipped, his hand sliding up and down her spine.

She tingled everywhere his hands touched her, and in other, more interesting places as well. "Sounds...promising," she said, adopting a sultry voice she hoped was filled with sin rather than the sudden case of nerves she felt.

He dipped his head, and traced his warm tongue

along that sensitive spot behind her ear. "Sweetheart, there's only one thing I want to promise you tonight."

She shivered, suppressing the moan of pleasure bubbling up inside her. "Such as?"

His teeth grazed the lobe of her ear. "To take you to the stars," he whispered, his hot breath fanning the flames already starting to lick through her.

Without a doubt she knew he wasn't referring to a moonlit stroll along the wharf. He'd made it abundantly clear he was speaking in the metaphorical sense this time...a journey straight to heaven.

CAIT TRIED not to flinch at the solid click of the door behind her, or the sound of Jordan turning the dead bolt, and failed.

"Would you like something to drink?" she asked nervously. She slipped off her wool coat and hung it in the closet, needing something to do with her trembling hands.

"All right," he said. She thought she detected a hint of amusement in his voice, but when she turned to look at him, he was all seriousness.

Not knowing what else to say, she nodded, then headed into the dining room for a bottle of wine, glasses and the silver serving tray, followed by a quick stop in the kitchen for some cheese. By the time she returned to the den, Jordan had a fire burning in the hearth. He'd tossed his jacket over the back of the love seat and loosened his tie, looking every inch the relaxed male. It wasn't fair, she thought. She was strung so tight, she was afraid she'd snap in two if he so much as touched her.

His welcoming grin, just a tad wicked, did little to

lessen her nervousness, nor did his fingers brushing hers when he took the tray from her and set it on the cocktail table. He straightened and looked at her. "Cait, are you nervous?"

She thought about lying, but she'd done enough of that with him already she didn't want to push her luck. "A little," she admitted.

Okay, a lot. She'd been a little nervous when they walked into the house, but the romantic stage he'd set had increased her nervousness, which was silly when she thought about it, especially after everything they'd already done this week.

His grin widened. "Come here," he ordered gently.

She did, and he captured both of her hands in his. "Your fingers are like ice." He covered hers to generate warmth.

"It was cold outside."

"We were in a heated vehicle," he countered teasingly.

She shrugged. "You know what they say about cold hands." She tried to manage a sultry tone, but all that came out was a hushed whisper. When he was looking at her with that burning intensity, she was lucky she could form a coherent thought, let alone speak aloud like a reasonable adult.

He let go of her hands, and skimmed his up her arms to her shoulders to gently guide her down to the sofa. Reaching into the pocket of his trousers, he pulled out a small, red velvet, heart-shaped jeweler's box.

Her heart thundered in her chest when he sat beside her. "Happy Valentine's Day," he said, holding the box in the palm of his hand.

She was afraid to take it, then mentally shook herself. Good grief, he wasn't proposing. And there was no engagement ring in that box either. To prove her point, she smiled weakly and lifted the box carefully from his palm.

Easing open the box, she gasped in surprise. Nestled against the red velvet lining sat a pair of earrings. The setting resembled a flower, with a small cluster of tiny diamond and emerald chips for the stem and leaves, and a delicate pearl at the center of each.

"They're beautiful," she said, unable to keep the delighted smile from her face. No one had ever given her such a thoughtful gift, but that wasn't the cause of her happiness. *Jordan* had given her these earrings. Because he'd given her back the money she'd paid him, she knew this wasn't part of some fantasy. This was real. "Thank you."

"Put them on," he said.

Grinning, she started to remove the plain gold hoops she'd worn.

"Cait?"

She slipped the first hoop from her lobe and glanced in his direction.

His eyes darkened. "Only those."

Her fingers stilled and her mouth went dry as dust. She'd known they were going to make love tonight. After the way she'd been practically begging him to all week, she supposed she'd be more than a little disappointed if they didn't go the distance. She just hadn't expected to feel so blasted nervous about it all, not after the way she'd been behaving all along.

"Here?" The gold hoop slipped from her fingers and dropped onto the cream velvet of her dress.

"We have a fire to keep us warm." He smoothed one hand over her knee as he reached behind her to snap off the lone lamp. The flames from the hearth cast the room in dancing shadows, further setting the stage for romance.

"We have wine to satisfy our thirst," he said, his fingers gently caressing the inside of her leg just above her knee. He leaned close, his hand sliding farther up her thigh.

"And we have each other to pleasure."

As if he'd poured warmed honey over her skin, her body instantly heated. Carefully sliding the second gold hoop from her lobe, she dropped it in her lap with the other, then removed Jordan's gift from the velvet bed. It took every ounce of concentration she possessed to insert the earrings, since his fingers were trailing a heated path up her thigh.

She finished putting on the earrings and glanced in his direction. His eyes darkened and a rascal's grin curved his mouth, and then he moved from beside her and crouched in front of her. Using his hands, he pressed her thighs open and pushed the hem of her dress up to expose the tops of her lacy nylons. His fingers smoothed over the lace, lightly brushing her exposed skin, reaching farther up to the satin edge of her teddy. She felt restless inside, and she needed to touch him, wanting him to feel the same tight, achy sensations his simple touch created inside her.

His gaze held her mesmerized while his hands gripped her hips and eased her toward the edge of the sofa. When his mouth finally claimed hers, he kissed her long and deep, hot and wet, sliding his tongue over hers in that ancient rhythm foretelling a more intimate mating.

She felt the brush of cool air against her back and realized he'd somehow undone the pearl buttons of her dress, then he slowly peeled the velvet from her skin. He urged her bottom up and worked the dress from her, slipping off her pumps as well, leaving her wearing nothing but the eggshell satin teddy and her nylons.

He eased away from her and stood, removing his shirt and tie. "Stand up," he ordered in sensual demand.

She complied, and then he turned her around so her back was flush with the wide expanse of his chest. He slid his hands over her breasts, down the satin of her teddy, his fingers stopping an inch shy of where she wanted him to touch her the most.

"Kneel on the cushion."

She did as he asked without question. He could have commanded her to strip and dance for him, and she would have done it if it meant more of the heated, sensual delights rippling through her.

He pressed against her back, his hands moving up her sides to her arms. Taking her hands, he guided them to the back of the sofa. His warm breath caressed her neck as he bit and nipped his way down her back. Using his tongue, he traced her spine while his hands slid down her sides and over her stomach.

Heat pooled in her belly and lower, and she arched her back. Her bottom pressed against the soft fabric of his trousers and she knew in an instant he was as aroused as she. Making love to him was going to be the single most beautiful experience of her life, she'd never doubted that for a second. She hadn't expected it to be the most erotic and sensual as well.

He must have sensed her growing need, because he slipped his hand over her most intimate place. The combination of his gentle, erotic touch and the slick satin made her cry out, then moan as he tugged the snaps of her teddy and eased his finger deep inside her dampened center. She pressed against his hand and her bottom rubbed evocatively against the erection straining his trousers.

"You're so wet," he murmured against her ear, his hot breath fanning her neck.

"I want you inside me," she demanded. She needed him, needed him to cool the flames licking through her. She moved slightly, widening her kneeling stance.

He sucked in a sharp breath when she pressed against him again, her body demanding fulfillment. One hand caressed her bottom, while the other continued the more sensual exploration. His fingers slid deep inside, then retreated to circle and tease, causing the tightening in her belly to increase.

"Jordan," she cried as he expertly drew her closer to the edge where heaven awaited. And then he stopped and she thought she'd die.

Turning her, he eased her down on the sofa and slipped the teddy from her body. "You are so beautiful. I need to taste you," he murmured, his mouth blazing a trail of heat over her stomach and down.

He pressed her thighs open and urged her bottom to the edge of the sofa. Running his hands over her legs, he carefully settled them over his shoulders. His tongue circled her navel, dipping lower until he kissed her intimately.

She gripped the edge of the sofa as the orgasm just out of her reach inched nearer. His tongue slid over and around, tasting, loving and kissing her deeply and passionately. She didn't think she could stand another minute of the erotic lovemaking when the orgasm finally slammed into her, making her call his name and tremble with the tiny tremors that shook her.

The wave passed as quickly as it had crashed through her, and she greedily wanted more. She wanted Jordan inside her, wanted to make him feel the same wondrous sensations. She didn't have long to wait. He stood and removed the rest of his clothing, then took care to protect her before lifting her off the sofa and carrying her to the soft, oriental carpet before the fire.

He stretched out beside her, running his hands over her skin as he kissed her again before easing his large body over hers. She wreathed her arms around his neck and held him close. Using his elbows for support, he slid his hands into her hair, then slid into her.

She closed her eyes and lifted her hips to meet him.

"Open your eyes," he demanded hoarsely. "I want to see your eyes when you come for me this time, sweetheart."

She did, and reveled at the tenderness cast within his own. Loving Jordan was so easy, she thought, as his body re-created the magnificent sensations destined to carry her to the heavens once again.

"I love you," she whispered, hoping he'd remember those three special words in the morning when she confessed the truth. She should have been honest with him before they made love. Anything else was selfish and self-serving, and for that she was incredibly sorry. But nothing, not even the threat of never seeing Jordan again, could make her utter the words now that would destroy the culmination of magic between them.

"I know just how you feel," he said softly in that velvet tone she'd never be able to forget.

She gave herself up to the heat and the emotion shining in his eyes, and when she came, she did so knowing for one brief moment, she'd known the meaning of true love. And she'd found it in her valentine's arms.

12

JORDAN COULDN'T THINK of a better way to spend a Sunday morning than watching the woman of his dreams cook him bacon and pancakes wearing nothing but a contented smile and a short, satin robe, both of which he'd given her. Considering the extent of their nocturnal activities, he wasn't ashamed to admit he'd worked up one monster of an appetite.

When she opened a cabinet and reached toward the top shelf, the hem of the robe inched upward, exposing the shapely curve of her backside, sending a shot of desire ricocheting through him.

"Let me," he said, rising from the glass-topped table.

"I got it," she said, standing on tiptoe, but still coming up short of her goal.

He sidled up behind her and purposefully pressed against her, smiling to himself when she wiggled her bottom provocatively. Her voracious appetite would be the death of him yet but, man, what a way to go.

He gripped her hip in one hand to still her sensual torment, no matter how enticing, then reached over her to the platter she'd been attempting to pull from the cabinet.

Slowly, she turned in his arms, sliding her body along his until he ached to have her again. His hunger for her outweighed his need for sustenance when her lips curved in a deliciously wicked grin. "You're pretty handy to have around, McBride."

"Not just in the kitchen, either." He pulled her flush against him. Her full breasts pressed against his chest and he cursed the barrier of the curve-hugging satin he'd been admiring only moments ago. God, he wanted her, and was beginning to think he'd never get enough of her.

She pushed aside his unbuttoned shirt and slid her hands over his middle to wrap her arms around his waist. She smiled up at him, a mischievous twinkle in her eyes. "The variety of your talents astound me, Mr. McBride."

"I'll show you mine if you show me yours," he teased, dipping his head to nuzzle her neck.

She angled her head to give him better access, her breath escaping with a soft sigh. "My social calendar's remarkably empty today," she said, smoothing her hands over his back. "Where would you like to start?"

The pop of grease from the frying pan caught his attention and he lifted his head. "How about with my driving skills?"

She frowned. "Driving skills? As in get dressed and leave the house?"

He smoothed his thumb over the frown creasing her forehead. "There are a couple of newer housing developments I'd like to check out. What do you say?"

She let out a puff of breath that ruffled her bangs. "Oh, I suppose," she groused. "But I'd rather test your cuddling skills."

He chuckled. "We'll come home early and cuddle." He placed a quick, hard kiss on her sweet mouth. "I promise."

Cait reluctantly stepped out of Jordan's arms and poured herself another cup of coffee. After the things they'd done to each other until the wee hours of the morning, she was half-surprised she wasn't more uncomfortable around him in the light of day. But then again, considering their adventurous lovemaking, shyness would be a bit hypocritical at this point.

She removed the bacon from the frying pan and set it on the napkin she'd placed over the platter, while Jordan poured himself a second cup of coffee.

"I should call Austin," he said, propping his backside against the counter beside her. "If the situation was reversed, I'd be ticked at him for not letting me know where he'd been all night."

She smiled at Jordan's thoughtfulness. "I'm sure he has a pretty good idea." She added a drop of bacon grease to the griddle. "There's a phone in the den if you want some privacy."

He set his cup on the counter next to hers and sauntered out of the kitchen. A sudden ache filled her as she watched him walk away. All night long she'd discovered the beauty and the many secrets of the long, hard length of his body. She'd reveled in the ecstasy they'd created, and the emotion driving them both. Not only had they sought and received pleasure, they'd shared that special magic that only two people who cared deeply for each other could.

With a sigh, she poured batter onto the hot griddle, then turned to pull the silverware from the drawer, wondering if she had the strength, or even the courage, to destroy so soon whatever was happening between them. She had to, she decided, using her hip to close the drawer. The deception had gone on long enough. If she had any hope at all of sustaining a relationship with Jordan, she had to tell him.

No more excuses.

No more delays.

Now.

After flipping the pancakes, she crossed the kitchen to the table. She arranged the silverware on bright yellow place mats, glancing up as Jordan walked back into the kitchen.

One look at the hardness in his eyes, cold as marble, and her dreams of happily ever after shattered. Butterflies the size of pelicans took flight in her stomach. His granitelike expression could mean only one thing...he *knew*.

She straightened and gripped the back of the kitchen chair in front of her, wrapping her fingers around its wooden slat. "I'm not writing the story."

He tossed the manila folder labeled Fantasy for Hire on the table. The folder, which she must have left out by mistake when she hurried to meet her sisters yesterday, slid across the glass surface, the damning evidence fluttering to the floor at her feet.

"What the hell is going on?" he demanded in a voice cold enough to send a chill skating down her spine.

"Sit down, Jordan," she said, surprised her voice sounded so calm when her insides where nothing but a jittery mass of nerves.

"I don't want to sit down," he barked at her. He crossed his arms over his chest and regarded her with such loathing her heart ached. "What's going on here? Who are you? God, is Cait even your real name?"

"Cait Sullivan is my name. I'm a reporter for the *San Francisco Herald.*"

"You lied to me. The entire time. It's been nothing but a lie."

She sucked in a deep breath and let it out slowly, praying she could make him understand that what had begun as lies and deceit had turned into something honest and pure. "I didn't have a choice."

"Everyone has choices," he continued gruffly. "It's what you do with those choices that determines your fate."

"Jordan, please," she said, lifting her hand toward him, but his harsh glare had her stuffing her hands in the side pockets of her robe instead. "Sit down and let me explain."

He moved suddenly, and she thought for a moment he would sit and they could discuss the issue rationally, but he stepped around her to the sliding glass door overlooking the ornamental garden. He didn't say anything for a moment, just stood there with his hands braced on his hips.

"Why should I believe anything you have to say?" he asked in an even tone. Before she could answer, he spun around and pinned her with that icy stare. "Everything," he said, his voice rising, "everything between us has been a lie."

"No," she cried. "I mean, yes. Not really."

"Which is it? Or have you told me so many lies you don't even know what the truth is any longer?"

She winced at his words, but they were no more

than she deserved. "At first I was trying to get information about the agency, but I wasn't lying when I told you I loved you. You have to believe that."

The iciness surrounding him numbed her soul. She fought back a rush of tears as the truth settled over her. Just as she'd feared, her declaration of love hadn't been enough.

"I want the truth," he demanded in the same angry tone. "All of it. Now."

"Initially, you were a story. I received a tip that your brother's agency was into fulfilling more than just fantasies, that it was bilking wealthy clients out of money in exchange for sex."

He said nothing, just continued to stare at her with enough loathing to make her weep. "I came up with a plan to go undercover and investigate the lead," she admitted around the lump forming in her throat. "I never planned on falling in love with you."

"Why didn't you just ask me about the agency?" he asked, purposely ignoring her more tender declaration. "I would have told you anything you wanted to know."

"Not if you really were running an illicit operation. Would you really have admitted that to a reporter?" She shook her head and continued. "The only way I could get the information I needed was to use myself as bait.

"I'm not rich, Jordan, not by a long shot. This isn't even my house. It's my brother, Brian's, and I've been house-sitting for him. That financial portfolio you saw is a fake too. I have exactly twenty-three hundred and forty-two dollars in the bank, and that's only because I deposited the money you gave back to me."

"What did you hope to gain?"

"By pretending to be rich and willing, I was supposed to be the perfect target for the agency. If the agency really was into that kind of thing, you wouldn't have been able to resist the temptation of my supposed fortune."

He crossed his arms over his chest again and regarded her speculatively. At least he was willing to listen, she thought, giving her hope that maybe he'd be willing to forgive her.

"Whatever gave you the crazy idea that my brother was ripping off women?"

"Louden Avery came into my office with a tip for a story. He told me that a wealthy employee of his had paid Fantasy for Hire and that the agency had taken her money in exchange for sex. When I first started this, I had no idea that Theodora Spencer was the employee. I didn't even know they called her Teddy until last night when you told me. But it didn't matter because I'd already decided not to write the story."

He shook his head, as if he couldn't believe what she'd just told him. "Looks like I wasn't the only one taken for a fool," he said.

"What do you mean?"

"My sister-in-law originally hired Austin to be her fiancé to keep Avery from sexually harassing her. Her girlfriends had hired the agency for Teddy's birthday. She was up for a promotion, but Avery kept making these snide little innuendos, and Teddy was uncomfortable. She'd fabricated a fiancé to get the bastard off her back, but that only worked for so long, and when Avery pressed her for a name, she blurted

Austin's and then hired him to be her fiancé for her company Christmas party."

"How did Avery find out the truth?"

"His secretary recognized Austin from some bachelorette party and told Avery. From what Teddy told us, he went snooping and found the receipt for the money she'd paid Austin, then threatened her. She stood up to him, and he was finally found out by the brass and fired. Seems Teddy wasn't the only one he'd attempted to victimize."

Cait dropped onto the bar stool, unable to believe she'd been duped. Now she knew what had been bothering her all along, that vital missing piece she'd needed hadn't been waiting for her in the Fantasy for Hire office, but rather with her source. Now she understood Avery's desperation for her to expose the agency…to exact his revenge on Teddy.

She dropped her head into her hands, shocked that her ambition had allowed her to be so gullible. "God, I've been such a fool."

"You weren't the only one," he said, the sharpness creeping back into his voice.

She looked up, but he wouldn't look at her. Instead, he strode past her as if she no longer existed and disappeared upstairs.

She couldn't let him leave like this. She had to make him understand. She found him upstairs, sitting on the edge of the king-size bed, his elbows braced on his knees, staring at the carpet between his feet.

"No, Jordan," she said quietly, crossing the plush carpet to stand before him. "You're wrong. It might have started that way, but I fell in love with you. I think I fell in love with you that night on the wharf. No one has ever—"

He looked up, his angry gaze locking with hers. "Come off it, Cait," he said with contempt. "The charade is over. Only you didn't get what you wanted, did you? Using me didn't gain you a damn thing. Well, I have news for you, sweetheart," he said, coming up off the bed to tower over her. "Write that story and I'll make damn sure Teddy and Austin sue you and your paper so fast no one will even hire you to write for the back of cereal boxes."

"I already told you, I'm not writing the story. I knew a few days ago I was shelving it."

"Then why keep playing me for a fool?" he roared. "You could have told me the truth."

"I tried," she rallied, her voice rising in frustration. "I told you I wasn't who you thought I was, and you didn't take me seriously."

"You could have insisted," he said, dropping onto the edge of the bed again. He scooped up his socks and shoved his feet into them.

"Right, Jordan," she countered, planting her hands on her hips. "When exactly was I supposed to do this?"

He finished putting on his socks, then slipped on his loafers. "Last night would have been a good time."

"Really? And when was that? When my parents were cutting their anniversary cake, or when you were seducing me on the dance floor?"

He stood and gave her a look filled with loathing before crossing the room to the bureau. "Seduce you?" He laughed, the sound cruel and caustic.

"You're the one who's been trying to seduce me all week long. But that was just part of your game, wasn't it?"

"No! It stopped being a game a long time ago."

"When did you come to this brilliant conclusion?" he asked bitingly.

She wrapped her arms around her middle, but it did little to stop her heart from breaking. "The night you gave me a bubble bath. I knew then that it was you I wanted and not the story, but I couldn't let it go," she admitted shamefully. God, she couldn't believe she'd been so foolish. Jen had been right all along. And now, just as her closest friend had predicted, she was losing Jordan.

He stuffed his wallet into his hip pocket, then scooped his change off the dresser. "You should have told me, Cait."

"I'm sorry."

"There's one thing I don't understand," he said, buttoning his shirt. "Why go to such lengths for a story? What were you hoping to get out of this?"

She closed her eyes, knowing what she was about to say would be the final stake through the heart of their relationship.

"A promotion," she said quietly.

He swore viciously, then spun on his heel and stormed out of the bedroom. She followed him down the stairs and into the den. She didn't know what to say to make him understand she'd never meant to hurt him like this. He scooped his keys off the cocktail table and snatched his jacket from the love seat where he'd left it the night before.

He was hurting and she was responsible. She was

no better than the partners in the firm who'd used him for their own financial gains. God, she'd give anything to take back the pain she'd caused him. She completely understood that pain, because she felt it clear to the bottom of her soul.

He walked past her, but she reached out to stop him. He looked down at her hand clasping his arm as if he couldn't bear to have her touch him. "I didn't mean to hurt you, Jordan."

He pulled his arm away, and for the first time ever, she knew real heartache.

"You can't hurt me, Cait. I don't care about you enough to let you hurt me."

The tears she'd been struggling to hold back since he'd found the file blurred her vision. "You don't mean that," she said around the burning lump lodged in her throat. "Not after what we shared last night. I know you don't mean that."

He laughed, the sound cold and hollow. "Just another part of the fantasy, babe. Courtesy of Fantasy for Hire."

DISGUSTED, Jordan tossed the colored pencil into the tray just as the telephone in Austin's office rang again, interrupting his concentration. Not that he'd been able to concentrate anyway, he thought grumpily. He crumpled the sketch he'd been working on into a ball and tossed it in the garbage can. Since he'd walked out on Cait a little over a week ago, his concentration had been at a minimum, something he couldn't afford now that he had so much work to do.

He pushed away from his art table and strode to the window overlooking the street below. With his hands shoved into the pockets of his trousers, he gazed at the sun just beginning to dip below the horizon, the brilliant red and gold reminding him too much of the fiery redhead he couldn't get out of his mind, or his heart.

The passage of a week didn't lessen his anger, but at least he could look at the situation dispassionately. Not even Cait could take full blame for playing him for a fool, because he'd allowed her to do it by ignoring the signs along the way. He'd been so wrapped up in her, he'd foolishly believed the series of inconsistencies were nothing more than personality quirks. Her slip about the dog shows, or the way she pinched pennies by refusing to pay for parking. But the worst of it was, he'd believed her when she'd said she loved him.

Because you chose to believe her.

With a growl of frustration, he left the room he'd been using as his temporary office and headed downstairs just as Austin walked through the front door.

"What'd you do?" Jordan asked, taking his cranky mood out on his unsuspecting brother. "Put a buy-one-get-one-free ad in every newspaper in the city?"

Austin crouched to untie his muddy work boots. "What are you talking about?"

Jordan ignored the knowing smirk on his brother's face. If he so much as complained about the weather lately, Austin blamed it on the breakup with Cait, and took a little too much joy in reminding him.

"The phone's been ringing off the hook while I've been trying to work. Do you know how distracting it is to hear that incessant noise all day long?"

Frowning, Austin walked into the office to the answering machine. His eyes rounded in surprise. "What the..." He dropped into the chair and punched the button. Fifteen minutes later, he sat back and looked over the desk at Jordan in confusion. "What are these women talking about? I didn't place any ad in the paper. Fantasy for Hire doesn't advertise. We're strictly a word-of-mouth operation."

Jordan leaned back in the metal folding chair across the desk from Austin and kicked his feet up on the corner of the scarred wood. "You sure? I counted thirty-two calls."

"Thirty-six," Austin said, glancing down at the schedule. "I bet it was Don. He's the employee who bought the business from me. Since he's taking over the first of the month, maybe he placed an ad."

"That doesn't make any sense," Jordan reasoned, folding his hands over his abdomen. "Not when you receive a percentage of any bookings from now until he officially takes over the business."

"It's not an ad."

Both men looked up to see Teddy standing in the doorway, a copy of the *San Francisco Examiner* in her hands.

Jordan swore softly, and received one of those looks from his sister-in-law that would make any grammar-school teacher proud. "I warned that—"

"You've been stomping around this house for the better part of ten days, Jordan McBride," Teddy interrupted, the trace of steel in her sweet voice matching the sudden hardness in her dark brown eyes. "And it's time you stopped."

"Honey, I don't think you should interfere."

"You keep quiet," she told Austin sternly, "because you're just as responsible."

"Me?" Austin looked affronted. "Don't blame me because he's been Grumpy the Bear."

"Did you or did you not fail to tell Jordan everything he needed to know about running Fantasy for Hire in your absence?"

Jordan swung his feet to the floor and stood. "It doesn't matter. She used me. I can't forgive that."

Teddy dropped the newspaper on the desk. "The least you could do is read her article."

He shoved his hands in his pockets. "Why? So I can see her lies in print? I don't need to see what I already know."

Teddy crossed her arms and regarded him with a tilt of her head. "What is it with you McBride men?"

"Hey, now—"

She shot Austin a look that had him raising his hands in defeat. To Jordan, she said, "Are you really willing to throw away a once-in-a-lifetime chance at happiness because Cait was smart enough, and determined enough, to try to get what she wanted?"

"She used me, Teddy."

Teddy shrugged her slim shoulders. "Maybe she did, but I used Austin. Does that make me a bad person?"

Austin slid a ledger from the metal tray. "I was your willing victim, honey."

Despite her serious demeanor, a grin briefly tugged her lips. "If you really think about it, I used him to get what I wanted. I wanted the promotion to senior graphic designer and I used Austin to keep

Louden away from me. How is that any different than what Cait did?"

"You told Austin up front what you wanted. Cait wasn't that honest."

"Oh. I see. So even though my motives weren't any more honorable than Cait's, what I did is acceptable because I let Austin in on my scam."

"You didn't lie to Austin," Jordan argued.

"No, what I did was much worse. I lied *about* Austin. I was embarrassed by what I thought he did for a living, so I fabricated a career for him. I didn't have any faith in him, which in my opinion is a much more serious offense. Cait always believed in you."

"What makes you say that?"

Teddy slipped out of her plaid wool blazer and tossed it over the chair. "I talked to her. She's left the *Herald* and she called me before she took the article to press with the *Examiner*."

Austin leaned back in the leather chair, lacing his fingers behind his head. "Give it up, big brother," he laughed. "You're not going to win. I've been married less than a month, and I learned real quick that I'm never going to win another argument for as long as I live."

Teddy slipped a strand of her shoulder-length blond hair behind her ear and perched her hip against the edge of the desk before giving Austin a sassy grin filled with affection. Then she turned back to Jordan. "Don't let your pride stop you from being happy, Jordan. I almost did, and I was miserable."

What if Teddy was right? Was his pride getting in the way of what he really wanted: a lifetime with Cait?

He slid the newspaper from the desk and left the office, his sister-in-law's words ringing in his ears. After pouring himself a cup of coffee, he sat at the kitchen table and unfolded the paper to the human-interest section.

HIRED HUNKS
WHAT'S *YOUR* FANTASY?

Tall, dark and gorgeous isn't just for fairy tales or wishful girlhood dreams a y longer. Fantasy for Hire, a San Francisco agency specializing in male exotic dancers, isn't your average, run-of-the-mill service of boy-toys taking off their clothes for a price. No, ladies, break out the checkbooks, because this agency specializes in something far more lasting...true love!

Jordan read Cait's article about Austin and Teddy's romance and how Fantasy for Hire was responsible for bringing them together. Each paragraph, combined with the firm reminder of Teddy's words, effectively chipped away at his pride. He also read the accompanying piece on the civil lawsuit brought against Louden Avery for sexual harassment by a number of women at the ad agency where Teddy still worked. By the time he finished he knew what he had to do...even if it meant groveling.

He tucked the newspaper away, grabbed his keys and headed for the front door.

"Hey, where are you going?" Austin called from the office.

Jordan walked into the office, almost offended by

the smug I-told-you-so smile canting his sister-in-law's lips.

"To ask for Cait's forgiveness," he said, returning Teddy's smile with one of his own.

"Don't forget the knee pads. You're going to need them for all that begging you'll be doing," Austin teased.

"What are you going to do?" Teddy asked after she swatted playfully at her recalcitrant husband.

"Create the ultimate fantasy," Jordan said, tossing his keys into the air. "And hope like hell it works."

"ARE YOU SURE this is for me?" Cait asked the courier.

The teenage boy snapped his gum. "You Cait Sullivan?"

"Yes."

"Then it's for you. Sign here," he said and thrust a metal clipboard into her hands.

She signed her name on the line he indicated, then took the thick manila envelope from him. Closing the door, she carried the envelope into the den and sat on the edge of the sofa.

She opened it and pulled out a copy of the newspaper where she now worked as a field reporter covering the legal beat. Instead of spending endless hours at boring social functions, her days were spent at the San Francisco Superior Court building.

She looked down at the newspaper. Written across the front in black marker in a bold scrawl she instantly recognized were instructions to turn to page F5. Her hands trembled as she opened the *Examiner* to the appropriate section. There was no need to scan the page since he'd circled the personal ad.

C.S.: Come to the wharf as you are. Go to the last shop on the left and ask for Elaine. Love, J.M.

Her heart pounded painfully behind her ribs as she read the personal ad again.

Love, J.M.

She wanted to weep with joy. When she'd called Teddy McBride last week to discuss the article with her, her intent had been to expose Louden Avery. When Teddy insisted on meeting with her, she'd reluctantly agreed, and after a couple of mai tais, it hadn't taken much prompting for the other woman to wrangle the truth out of her.

By the time they left the Frisco Bay Bar, Teddy had been confident that Jordan would forgive her, provided Cait handled him just right. The McBride men were more than stubborn, she'd said. They were impossible, but worth every ounce of effort.

Taking the newspaper with her, Cait drove to the wharf and hurried down the pier to the shop Jordan indicated. The shop was of the New Age variety, filled with crystals, herbs, oils and other potions all proclaiming certain powers.

The bell above the door jangled as she stepped inside and walked to the counter. Scents mingled, but the odor was more pleasing than pungent. A tall, reed-thin woman behind the counter greeted her with a warm smile.

"I'm supposed to see Elaine."

The woman's smile widened. "Miss Sullivan?" At Cait's nod, she said, "I've been expecting you." She reached beneath the counter and retrieved a heavy floral bag with twin hoop handles.

Cait opened the bag and pulled out a small vial of aromatherapy oil. Twisting off the cap, she breathed in the scent, a mixture of rose and other fragrances she couldn't identify. "What is it?" she asked the saleswoman.

"This is our most popular oil," she said. The cluster of bangle bracelets on the woman's wrists jangled as she mixed a herbal concoction. "It's a blend of rose, lavender, vanilla and basil with just the right touch of honeysuckle that opens your heart to love and joy and allows you to express heartfelt emotions and romantic desires."

Cait couldn't have prevented the huge grin curving her lips if she'd tried, or have been more touched by Jordan's romantic gesture. When she'd gone with him to the wharf and they'd ventured into the shop, he'd been skeptical about the power the aromatherapy oils, crystals and other unique gifts contained.

"Your young man left a note," Elaine said, then turned her attention back to her herb blending.

Cait thanked the woman and left the shop, waiting until she was outside before retrieving the small white card from inside the bag.

A small side trip is necessary for this fantasy to be complete. Go to 4459 Canter...and hurry!

Surely he didn't intend to have her traipsing around San Francisco all afternoon, she thought as she headed to the next destination. She entered a liquor store where the clerk handed her a bottle of champagne and a pair of plastic cups along with one more note promising fulfillment soon.

When she arrived at the next designated location, a florist presented her with an enormous spring bouquet and a map directing her to the outskirts of the city.

The Saturday-afternoon traffic was heavy, and by the time she located the area, her patience was starting to wear thin. She pulled into a cul-de-sac still under development, found Jordan's 4X4 parked in the unfinished driveway of one of the homes and parked her car.

Taking the oil, flowers and champagne with her, she carefully made her way across the dirt path framed by planks and up a set of wooden steps to the wraparound front porch. Taped to the brass knocker on a set of double oak doors was a note proclaiming:

Enter only if willing to accept the following terms: Happily ever after!

Cait didn't have to think twice. She pushed open the door and stepped into what would eventually resemble a foyer. Closing the door behind her, she stopped in the center of a large common area. Leaning against the wall waiting for her was her own special valentine, looking contrite, slightly nervous and sexier than any man had a right to.

"I was beginning to think you weren't going to come," he said, pushing off the wall to stroll slowly toward her. She set the gifts on a nearby scaffold and waited for him to close the distance between them, afraid to speak for fear of breaking whatever spell he was under.

His hand trembled slightly when he lifted it to run his knuckles gently over her cheek. Her heart melted.

"I love you, Cait." The emotion in his voice matched the tenderness of his gaze, touching her soul as only Jordan could. "I've been miserable without you. Please say you can forgive me for being such a jerk."

"I don't know," she said with a regretful shake of her head. "I mean, how can I wh—"

"Hey." His frown was instant and deep. "I know I was a jackass and I'm sorry—"

She placed her fingers over his lips to quiet him. "Let me finish, Jordan. How can I forgive you when there's nothing to forgive?"

He grasped her wrist in his large, warm hand. "Cait, I'm serious."

"So am I. I admit I did set out to deceive you, but I never meant to hurt you. When I walked into Fantasy for Hire, I never expected to fall in love with you."

A devilish light entered his eyes and his mouth quirked into one of those sexier-than-sin smiles that made her pulse race. "I'm just damned irresistible."

Cait laughed and looped her arms around his neck to pull him close. "And arrogant," she added teasingly. She lifted her lips to his for a kiss filled with tenderness and all the emotions she'd kept locked away since he'd walked out on her two weeks ago.

He ended the kiss and looked into her eyes. "I do love you," he said again, chasing away the doubts and fears that she'd lost him forever.

He pulled her arms from around his neck and plucked the champagne and cups from the scaffold.

Cait looked around the shell of the house. The

walls had been drywalled and taped, but not yet painted, and some were still in the framing stage. "Why are we here? Is this one of your designs?"

He grinned. "Not exactly. Come on. I'll give you a tour and you can tell me what you think."

She shrugged and ventured deeper into the home. Jordan led the way, explaining what was still to be done to complete each of the rooms, sometimes getting into a little too much detail, but she smiled and listened just the same. They wound their way up the staircase to the upper level and he showed her the bedrooms, ending the tour in an enormous master bedroom and what promised to be an elegant adjoining bath.

He set the glasses on the marble counter of the sink and worked the top off the champagne. "So, what do you think?"

"I think it's going to be absolutely gorgeous."

His grin widened. "What if I said it was yours?"

"What?"

"But, there's a catch," he added, slipping the foil off the champagne bottle.

She crossed her arms over her chest and regarded him carefully. The note *had* said happily ever after. "Which is?" she asked cautiously.

He casually twisted the wire securing the cork, taking care to hold it away from her. "You have to marry me to get the house."

Shock rippled through her and she stared at Jordan. She had no problem marrying the man. Spending the rest of her life with her own special fantasy-come-true was anything but a hardship. But...was he nuts?

"We can't possibly afford something like this." She closed the distance between them. "Jordan, my salary at the *Examiner* isn't quite as pitiful as what I was making at the *Herald*, but still... You're just starting your own business. We need to start out small. Couldn't we just rent an apartment for a few years? Once we have some serious money in savings...

"Why are you laughing?" she asked, convinced he'd lost his mind. "Money is a very serious matter."

He pulled her into his arms and gave her one of those bone-melting kisses that she looked forward to enjoying for the next sixty years. "Sweetheart," he said, kissing her jaw, her throat and finally nuzzling her ear. "We can afford it. Trust me."

"We can?"

He sighed and pulled her against him. "We can. There's the money from the condo in L.A., the business is taking off faster than I'd hoped and Austin and Teddy are buying me out of the Victorian."

"But I thought you'd never sell it."

"I wouldn't, except to sell my share to Austin and Teddy. It's their home now."

Keeping her tucked against his side, he handed her a plastic cup filled with champagne. "To the fantasy?"

She smiled up at him, and the love shining in his eyes warmed her soul. She touched her plastic cup to his and shook her head. "Not this time," she said. "This time it's to *happily ever after*."

_____ Epilogue _____

JORDAN PEERED over his brother's shoulder, careful to keep a safe distance. "Are you sure you know what you're doing?" he asked, hoping Cait didn't expect him to complete such a Herculean task on his own.

"Piece of cake," Austin said, securing the plastic tab over the front of the disposable diaper.

Jordan took a tentative step toward the sofa. "Aren't you supposed to use powder or something?"

"Teddy says it's best for the baby if you don't use anything." Austin smoothed the T-shirt over the infant's tummy. "Isn't it, sweetheart?" he crooned to his daughter.

Five-month-old Elizabeth McBride squealed and kicked her chubby legs while Austin competently slipped them back inside the pink terry-cloth sleeper, despite his daughter's rambunctious antics. Task complete, he scooped the little girl into his arms, then looked over his shoulder at Jordan.

"Don't worry, big brother," he said, his voice filled with a confidence Jordan actually admired. "It's not as hard as it looks."

Jordan failed to agree, but he supposed in about another three weeks he'd be discovering the truth of that statement for himself.

Jordan turned down the volume of the baseball game neither of them was watching. "Cait wants to do this again," he told his brother. "I sure wouldn't go through what she's suffered the past few weeks. If her feet aren't swollen, then her back's bothering her, or she's just plain exhausted."

Austin pulled a juice bottle from the diaper bag and effortlessly rearranged his daughter in his arms. "I feel for you. Teddy's already talking about having another one next year."

"Cait wants four," Jordan said, unable to stop the wicked grin from tugging his lips. He had to admit, the thought of giving Cait all those babies was definitely appealing.

Jordan watched Austin bottle-feed Elizabeth, smiling every time his niece issued one of those little sighs of contentment. Odd, he thought, but he just couldn't get used to thinking of his brother as a parent. It didn't seem all that long ago Austin was a rebellious teen, and Jordan's sole responsibility. For Teddy's sake, he hoped Elizabeth didn't give them half as much trouble as Austin had given him.

"What are you grinning about?" Austin asked.

"Just thinking about Elizabeth as a teenager," he said with a chuckle. "Good luck, little brother."

Austin's eyes narrowed in suspicion. "What's that supposed to mean?"

Jordan's laughter deepened. "It means that I sincerely hope neither one of you has to suffer what I did with you."

Austin leaned back against the pale green throw pillows. "You were bossy and wanted everything your way. Ever hear of a little thing called freedom?"

"About as much as you heard of a little thing called responsibility," Jordan countered.

"I was plenty responsible."

"Sure you were. That's why I found you necking up on the lookout right after you got your driver's license. And you were only sixteen."

A grin tugged Austin's lips. "Yeah, well, what were you doing up there? Sure as hell not studying for an astronomy exam."

The front door opened, followed by the sound of feminine voices, effectively ending the good-natured exchange.

"Mommy's home," Austin said to his daughter, setting the empty juice bottle on the cocktail table.

A quick jolt of pleasure shot through Jordan at the sight of Cait. She wore a loose cotton sundress that outlined the swell of her tummy, and despite her complaints to the contrary, he thought she looked stunning.

He frowned at the lines of fatigue bracketing her eyes, concern rippling through him when she pressed her hand against the small of her back.

He stood and crossed the room toward her. "Are you feeling all right?" he asked, slipping his arm over her shoulders, guiding her to the recliner.

She smiled up at him, lifting her lips for a kiss, which he quickly and happily obliged.

"I'm fine," she said, gently easing down into the chair. "There's a ton of stuff in Teddy's trunk. I think we hit every sale in the Bay Area today."

Teddy smiled as she lifted her daughter in her arms. "You've got everything you could possibly need for the baby."

Cait laughed and laced her fingers with Jordan's. "I'm sorry, Jordan, but Teddy's wrong. We have enough for ten babies." To Teddy, she asked, "How many clothes does one little baby need?"

Austin and Teddy looked at each other and smiled. "A lot," they said simultaneously and laughed.

CAIT CURLED onto her side, snuggling as close to Jordan as she realistically could, given her size. "I feel like a baby elephant," she complained in the darkness of the master bedroom. And to top if off, the doctor had ordered her to take it easy, which, according to Jordan, meant no sex. Something she planned on changing—effective immediately. She'd seduced him once, she could do it again.

"I think you're beautiful," he murmured, placing a light kiss on the top of her head.

"Hmmph," she muttered with a puff of exasperation. "Teddy and I were talking today..."

"Uh-oh," he said, his sleepy voice filled with humor.

"Did you know that Austin and Teddy made love until the day before Elizabeth was born?"

Her husband sighed heavily, but she wasn't about to be dissuaded from her course of action.

"In fact," she continued, "Dr. Hamilton told Teddy the same thing—to take it easy the last month. They ignored him."

"Probably because Teddy didn't tell Austin about Dr. Hamilton's instructions." He eased away and reached over her to turn on the lamp.

"Medieval edict, you mean," she complained grumpily.

Arranging the pillows against the headboard, he gave her a level stare. "Sweetheart," he said in a placating tone that was beginning to irritate her, "Dr. Hamilton's been delivering babies for thirty-five years—"

"Exactly my point," she argued, struggling to sit. Dammit, what was wrong with wanting to make love to her husband? She was pregnant for crying out loud, not terminal. "Jordan, this is the same man who delivered you and your brother. Don't you think he's being just a bit old-fashioned? And for the record, Teddy did tell Austin."

"I just think—"

"That's your problem, McBride," she groused, scooting off the edge of the king-size bed. "You're spending too much time thinking instead of taking action."

She circled the huge bed and stopped when she reached his side. He crossed his arms over his wide, bare chest, and her heart slammed into her ribs. She didn't think she'd ever grow complacent where her husband was concerned. Even after two and a half years of marriage, he could ignite the flames of desire with little effort. One look at the sensual glint in his eyes and she was ready, willing and more than able.

"What's that supposed to mean?" he asked, eyeing her warily.

"It means," she said, tossing back the covers and using every ounce of self-control she possessed to keep her gaze locked on her husband's face and not his gloriously nude body. She lost the battle and looked anyway.

"It means—" she cleared her throat and dragged her gaze up his torso to his lips and finally back to his caution-filled eyes "—that you, my darling husband, haven't been behaving too much like a fantasy lately."

Holding up the hem of her short, cotton nightgown, she climbed onto the bed and clumsily inched her way toward him on her knees. "I'm going to have to demand that you provide the services promised."

He reached out to steady her as she moved closer and straddled his hips. "Cait—"

"I thought customer satisfaction was your number-one priority."

The grin tugging his lips was nothing short of wicked. "So it's a fantasy you want, Mrs. McBride?"

She wiggled as close as her tummy would allow, smiling when he sucked in a sharp breath.

"Yes. I have a fantasy."

"And?"

She grinned. "And," she said, sifting her fingers through his hair. "It starts with a kiss. Something long and...hard." She wickedly smoothed her hands down his chest and over his stomach.

He sucked in another sharp breath when her fingers wrapped around him. Easing his hand up the inside of her thigh, he added, "And wet." His fingers brushed against the place she craved his touch.

"Very wet," she moaned, rocking her hips toward him.

"Is that all?" he asked, using his free hand to guide her mouth toward his.

"Uh-uh. There's more," she whispered, nipping at his lower lip, then soothingly gliding her tongue over the spot. "There's much more."

"When do you plan to demand this fantasy?" He trailed hot kisses along her jaw and zeroed in on that sensitive spot behind her ear, causing her to tremble in his arms.

She slid her hands into his hair and held him close. "For the rest of our lives, Mr. McBride," she told him, and then they played out the fantasy together.

Temptation

A spicy hot love story

BLAZE

Available in February 2000

IN TOO DEEP
by
Lori Foster
(Temptation #770)

Charlotte (Charlie) Jones was used to fighting for what
she wanted, and she wanted Harry Lonigan—big-time!
But the sexy P.I. was doing his best to deny the steamy
attraction between them. Charlie was the daughter of
his best friend and father figure so, to his mind, she
was off-limits. But as he worked with Charlie on
an embezzling case, Charlie worked on him.
Before he knew it, Harry was in too deep.

BLAZE! Red-hot reads from Temptation!

Available at your favorite retail outlet.

If you enjoyed what you just read,
then we've got an offer you can't resist!

Take 2 bestselling
love stories FREE!
Plus get a FREE surprise gift!

Back by popular demand are

DEBBIE MACOMBER's

Hard Luck, Alaska, is a
town that needs women!
And the O'Halloran brothers
are just the fellows
to fly them in.

Starting in March 2000 this beloved series returns
in special 2-in-1 collector's editions:

MAIL-ORDER MARRIAGES, featuring
Brides for Brothers and *The Marriage Risk*
On sale March 2000

FAMILY MEN, featuring
Daddy's Little Helper and *Because of the Baby*
On sale July 2000

THE LAST TWO BACHELORS, featuring
Falling for Him and *Ending in Marriage*
On sale August 2000

Collect and enjoy each MIDNIGHT SONS story!

Available at your favorite retail outlet.

HARLEQUIN®
Makes any time special ™

Visit us at www.romance.net   PHMS

Return to the charm of the Regency era with

GEORGETTE HEYER,

creator of the modern Regency genre.

Enjoy six romantic collector's editions with forewords
by some of today's bestselling romance authors,

**Nora Roberts, Mary Jo Putney,
Jo Beverley, Mary Balogh,
Theresa Medeiros and Kasey Michaels.**

Frederica
On sale February 2000
The Nonesuch
On sale March 2000
The Convenient Marriage
On sale April 2000
Cousin Kate
On sale May 2000
The Talisman Ring
On sale June 2000
The Corinthian
On sale July 2000

Available at your favorite retail outlet.

HARLEQUIN®
Makes any time special ™